Michele Slung is the editor of *I Shudder at Your Touch*, *Shudder Again*, *Slow Hand*, and *Fever*, along with many other anthologies. She lives in New York City and upstate New York.

seduce me

TWELVE EROTIC STORIES

EDITED BY

Michele Slung

A PLUME BOOK

PLUME
Published by Penguin Group
Penguin Group (USA) Inc., 375 Hudson Street, New York, New York 10014, U.S.A.
Penguin Group (Canada), 10 Alcorn Avenue, Toronto, Ontario,
Canada M4V 3B2 (a division of Pearson Penguin Canada Inc.)
Penguin Books Ltd., 80 Strand, London WC2R 0RL, England
Penguin Ireland, 25 St. Stephen's Green, Dublin 2, Ireland
(a division of Penguin Books Ltd.)
Penguin Group (Australia), 250 Camberwell Road, Camberwell,
Victoria 3124, Australia (a division of Pearson Australia Group Pty. Ltd.)
Penguin Books India Pvt. Ltd., 11 Community Centre, Panchsheel Park,
New Delhi – 110 017, India
Penguin Books (NZ), cnr Airborne and Rosedale Roads, Albany, Auckland 1310,
New Zealand (a division of Pearson New Zealand Ltd.)
Penguin Books (South Africa) (Pty.) Ltd., 24 Sturdee Avenue, Rosebank, Johannesburg
2196, South Africa

Penguin Books Ltd., Registered Offices: 80 Strand, London WC2R 0RL, England

Published by Plume, a member of Penguin Group (USA) Inc. This is an authorized reprint of
a hardcover edition published by Venus Book Club. For information address Venus Book
Club, 401 Franklin Avenue, Garden City, New York 11530.

First Plume Printing, July 2005
10 9 8 7 6 5 4 3 2 1

(P) REGISTERED TRADEMARK—MARCA REGISTRADA

LIBRARY OF CONGRESS CATALOGING-IN-PUBLICATION DATA

Seduce me : twelve erotic stories / by Michele Slung.
    p. cm.
    Contents: In her garden / by Mia Mason—The butler did it / by Theresa Roland—
Southern comfort / by Laurel Gross—Mama said / by Maura Anne Wahl—A taste of
Rebecca / by Susan St. Aubin—A guide to alien dating / by Leigh Ward—Life class / by
Georgi Mayr—In the dark / by Dana Clare—Let me help / by Beth Miller—Vanessa takes
wing / by Cansada Jones—Rising son / by Gracia McWilliams—Touching / by Susanna
Foster.
    ISBN 0-452-28638-7 (trade pbk.)
    1. Erotic stories, American. 2. Seduction—Fiction. I. Slung, Michele B., 1947–

PS648.E7S43 2005
813'.54—dc22   2004065032

Printed in the United States of America

Contents

Editor's Note

Seduction is a state of mind, usually with a population of two. But no matter how familiar its portal might seem, what lies beyond is always uncharted territory.

In this collection you will find stories by writers who have lent their erotic imaginations to the exploration of this mysterious place. And with just two words, the title manifests its unfailing allure.

Seduce me: is it an invitation or a command . . . or, somehow, both?

"Pursuit and seduction are the essence of sexuality," Camille Paglia has declared. Since I agree, I was startled when a few of the writers I contacted to contribute to *Seduce Me* begged to differ. "I don't usually do seduction stories," replied one. "I seem to prefer mutual lust."

It had never occurred to me that those two things might appear to be in opposition!

But when another potential contributor pointed out, "It seems like seduction is something different to everyone, and, especially, to women," I realized that I was learning on the job—just as I had been when I put together my first erotic anthologies, *Slow Hand* and *Fever*. Thus, in the stories that follow, the characters chart their own maps to the moment of seduction (and gratification), whether they are seducing or being seduced.

Here are some of the people you are about to meet: Rebecca, whose impulse visit to a piercing parlor turns unexpectedly hot; Martin, a butler whose upper lip isn't all that's stiff; Plum, a Japanese lady of pleasure with a mischievous yen for after-hours adventure; Karl, a young husband with a plan for arousing to distraction his domestic-goddess of a wife; Cara, whose blissful discovery of the perfect sex partner makes a kidnapping inevitable; and Drew, literally led down the garden path by a new neighbor to an extraordinary ecstatic encounter.

And if "most virtue is a demand for greater seduction," as Natalie Clifford Barney cleverly said, rest assured there is certainly a greater array of seduction on display in these pages than even the virtuous among you might require.

Think about the huge thrill of being excited by someone or exciting someone, with the accompanying promise and reality of foreplay in all its glory, whether verbal, physical, or spiritual.

Then, think about what comes next.

Then, I suggest you stop thinking.

for Mark

IN HER GARDEN

᷿

by Mia Mason

Drew knows wild irises smell sweeter than hybrids. He's done the sniff test on the light lavender blooms at the back of his property that are smaller than the exotic purple irises that came from his grandfather's hothouse, the ones his mother planted when they first moved here. Drew bought the house from his mother before she moved to Florida, mainly because of the wild irises.

He knows it's as goofy as hell to buy a house just for the sake of smelling those irises each spring, but that's what happened. Maybe it's because they remind Drew of his Uncle Pappy's drugstore candy counter and the sticky grape suckers he stole from a wide-mouthed jar when he thought Uncle Pappy wasn't looking.

But sometimes the wild iris scent takes him back to the pink cotton candy at the circus. The trapeze artists always amazed him—the incredible trust exhibited between partners flying through the air, hands reaching out and holding on for dear life, believing they'd be caught. The clowns he could skip, maybe. Scary bastards. And the monkeys in weird little suits and caps, and, oh yeah, the little poodles and other trick dogs jumping through hoops and stuff. They were cool, but what he loves the most is the memory of the cotton candy disintegrating into a sweet pink puff of nothing on his tongue. A bit like the scent of musky rose in the crotch of women's silk panties. He still keeps a pair of his old girlfriend Isabella's panties (and one pink Dior bra) in the lower drawer of his bureau. Sadly, her scent is fading.

In Kirsten's backyard—he knows her name is Kirsten something or other, he's seen it on her mailbox and in the neighborhood bulletin—wildflowers and tall grass compete with less wayward grass and ground cover. Creamy buttercups huddle together when a sudden north wind reminds them April has just given into May. And the wild irises rule there, too, but with one maddening difference—in Kirsten's yard they bloom a month earlier than his, and sometimes keep blooming through June!

In her backyard, everything blooms whenever it wants to, including honeysuckle, wisteria and jasmine vines. The wisteria by the fence they share is very eccentric. Drew noticed it blooming once in the dead of January, sending silvery purple blossoms scattering across his cracked patio. He's even caught a whiff of eucalyptus in December.

He has yet to really meet her. They've exchanged waves and grunts as they wheel their recycling and garbage out on

Monday mornings. What do you say over trash cans and bundles of papers? Me Tarzan. You Jane. I see my bin is bigger than your bin. Can I help you push yours to the curb?

Her dilapidated wooden stockade fence, basically, is being held up by his more practical chain-link fence. In places, the fence boards gape precariously. Knotholes and splintering spots provide ample opportunity to spy on her lovely but, let's face it, woefully overgrown yard. He doesn't like to think of himself as spying, but it's a temptation he gives into occasionally. Just to be friendly.

He hears her now moving around on her patio, among her flowers, blissfully rustling about among the clay pots she keeps filled with rosemary, basil and other herbs. The rosemary is the most pungent. Makes him a little hungry for roasted chicken. He can taste it, the juices dribbling on his fingers. Licking his fingers. Licking hers. His stomach growls. Rosemary chicken. Rosemary Kirsten.

He glances through a convenient knothole and glimpses a gloved hand flashing a trowel. By craning a bit to the left, he can see the tip of a bare foot in a thonged sandal adorned with a daisy. The toenails glisten a blushing taupe. "Hi, what're you planting today?"

He swears he can feel what it would be like if her toes tickled his bare toes. Why can't they be friends? A friendly yellow butterfly brushes past his head. His face flushes with absurd but hopeful expectation.

Today just feels special. The air seems electric. It's June. Anything can happen in June. June is when school's out.

Teachers and students on summer vacation. He teaches English Lit to juniors on the cusp of life. He feels like he's seventeen today. He rubs his stubbly chin. He should've shaved. Why didn't he shave? Weekends are meant for being lazy, right? He stares dubiously at the ancient Marilyn Manson T-shirt his nephew David gave him for Christmas, like, five years ago. Pathetic.

"Anyone there?" He curls a shoulder closer to the hole. "Hello?" He wonders what to say next. "Would you like to come over for a drink?"

She moved in about two years ago, but aside from their garbage encounters she's been as distant as the moon. He can't figure out why she's so aloof. It's not like she's J. Lo or Sandra Day O'Connor. He heard from Mrs. Gibson, the neighbor on his other side, that maybe she's a teacher or something with another local school district. He suspects Environmental Science or Biology?

Time to get real. They should meet.

He's lonely, and he bets she is, too. Maybe she's just shy. He thinks they're about the same age and he hasn't seen a regular guy hanging around. He's glimpsed her going to her utterly too cool, fuel-efficient hybrid car. He wonders if she'd speculated about him at all. What if she's some gangsta's lady, as David suggested in one of his mighty moronic moments? What if she prefers girls? He has to find out. Nice feet. Good toes.

She laughs teasingly. He strains to watch her take off the garden gloves slowly, one finger at a time, revealing small slender white hands. Her fingers plunge into the brown earth dotted with the white fertilizer granules. The pot appears to welcome her fingers as she gently settles a fuchsia-colored geranium into its new home. His eyes slide up her bare arm and the curve of her elbow and dances up to her bare shoulder. His neck pops as he contorts to follow the shoulder to a patch of her neck and then down to the gentle swell of her breasts, the pink nipples erect in the mild breeze.

Wait a minute! Is she buck naked? He backpedals, and falls down into a handy lawn chair. Damn! For a moment he is flabbergasted, stunned. Forget J. Lo, this is Madonna or Pamela Lee. He covers his mouth and contemplates his next move.

Her skin looks as soft as the wild roses that erupt in a cascade by his wind-weathered garage during May and June (that is, as long as he makes sure they get enough water). He stands back, amused by his own physical reaction to such a surprise.

Is she crazy? Is he? Should he say something else? Should he strip down and climb over the fence? Maybe he just imagined the whole thing. Surely she knows he's right there. Why doesn't she say something? He tears off his Marilyn Manson T-shirt and wipes his face. Damn! He rubs his chest and his own erect nipples startle him. Other changes in his body do not.

Maybe she really is Swedish or Danish—a Scandinavian import? Probably from Amsterdam. David's always going on about how he wants to go to Amsterdam.

"I hope you use sunscreen," Drew suddenly says, without thinking. Oh, that was witty. He hugs his bare chest and then suddenly wants desperately for it to be her hugging him.

She laughs again, a little slowly. Then she coughs. "I do," she says softly. "Do you?"

She must've looked through one of those knotholes. Damn. He straightens up. "Well, do you like what you see?"

As soon as he says this, he feels like the biggest dork in the universe. He wants to go inside her backyard and look into her eyes, but he also wants her to invite him in. He wouldn't, want to, like, trespass. He is a very good neighbor who does his bit for the neighborhood crime patrol. He also helped raise money to buy recreational items for the local kids' park, and he always picks up trash when he walks his dog, Marvin. Where is that dog, anyway?

He takes a breath and glances inside a knothole again. And sees that damn dog Marvin in her yard, wagging his tail with his tongue out! Double damn! "Kirsten, I am so sorry. I didn't know Marvin had got out and got over there to your yard. I'll come get him!" Bless that mongrel dog.

"Guess he wanted to sniff my daffodils," Kirsten says. He peeks again and sees her stroking his dog's fur. He feels a wave of jealousy. His daffodils didn't bloom in May. They were done in early March. It wasn't right that *she* still had daffodils blooming in April. It isn't fair. She's a gardening *goddess*. Drew shakes his head and grins.

Then he frowns. It's a warm day. He checks his armpits. Does he stink? Maybe he'd better go shower before he goes over there. Put on some deodorant? Aftershave? Maybe she has yellow irises, too. *She* probably has some frilly pale pink ones. He contemplated digging some up in the dark of night and transferring them to his backyard. But that would be stealing. Good neighbors did not steal.

Laughter. *She* was obviously doing something over there. Having fun with Marvin, the furry traitor. "I'll be there in a second. Have you had dinner? Want to order a pizza?" The words rush out of his mouth before he can dampen the excitement in his voice.

He looks through the hole again—surreptitiously, cautiously—and detects a flash of white by a pathway. White peonies, possibly. Big, fat, lacy petals fluttering. His mother used to love white peonies. His mother used to have a snowball bush by the side of the house, and some white peonies, too. She used to tend them so carefully, but he'd forgotten to have someone water them during a summer drought while he was on vacation in Mexico and they had died. It wasn't fair!

He crams his hands in his pockets and turns away. He waits for her voice. Will she say, "yes"? Then he hears a sound just on the cusp of music. Like someone trying to sing, and then stopping.

A sudden chill in the air makes his teeth chatter.

"Hello?" he says. "I'm waiting. So are you hungry? Are we on or not?"

A whisper greets his ears with a seductive, sibilant, "Absolutely, Drew—it is Drew, isn't it?"

"Kirsten, it is Kirsten, isn't it?"

Drew cranes his neck to see the green leaves rustle. Marvin barks, and Drew can see him in his mind's eye, shamelessly rolling around, tongue lolling out, exposing his belly, wanting it rubbed.

The wind tosses some wisteria petals across the fence. Drew wants *his* belly rubbed badly.

"Yes—Kirsten Freyja. And pizza sounds good. I'm very hungry and . . . you know what?"

He loves that word. "What?"

"We can eat here right on the patio!"

"I'll call in the order and be right over."

"No anchovies," Kirsten calls out. "But I like mushrooms and olives—green olives—and lots of garlic and cheese. And onions!" She sounds, like, fifteen.

"Onions and garlic?" His spirits sag.

"Oh yes. And I have some peppermint ice cream we can have for dessert. It cleanses the palate, no?"

She doesn't sound totally American. "You got beer?"

Silence.

"Wine?" What kind of wine do you drink with pizza?

"I have Italian bottled water and tap and some merlot," she tells him.

"Sure." He ducks into the house, hollering over his shoulder, "See you in a few minutes!" He hopes he doesn't sound too excited. He needs to calm down.

⬖⬗

He could've given her address to the pizza place, but he gave his, maybe as a way of buying time. His hands sweat as he grips the tops of his knees, the scent of his Ralph Lauren aftershave a bit heavy in the air of his living room. What was taking that delivery kid so long?

He imagines Kirsten in the shower preparing for his arrival, listening to Norah Jones or Enya, probably. Not the Dixie Chicks. Something European, slow, full of longing. Maybe some soundtrack from a French movie, like *Amélie*. He gets off on those French movies with subtitles. He likes to pretend he knows what they're saying. She probably speaks French and about four other languages.

And she probably uses those white nylon puffy things lathered up with lavender-scented soap. No, gotta be roses. Pink or coral roses. The steam rising in the air. Her hand reaching down to wipe her leg. Her thigh. Her. . . . Where is that pizza?

Pizza sounds so unromantic and messy for a first date. He imagines a string of mozzarella hanging off his chin. What a dumb idea. Chinese take-out in those little white boxes would've been better. With fortune cookies for dessert? He wasn't good at using chopsticks, and he bets she uses chopsticks like she was born in Taiwan. Delicate white fingers. He noticed she had a French manicure. And wasn't there a sliver of a bracelet on her wrist?

Was she wearing a ring?

Maybe she. . . .

The door buzzer sounds. It's about time.

Drew opens the door and gives the kid too much money. He holds the large box in his hand and suddenly realizes the scent of the oily pizza bottom will be on his hands when he arrives at her door. "Shit!" Too late now. She's hungry.

So is he.

He takes a deep breath and leaves. Should he go to the back or use the front door? He stands in between their two houses, glancing toward her backyard. He still can't believe she gardens in the buff.

The pizza box is hot.

"Kirsten, are you outside?" he calls out.

"Come around to my backyard, to the gate. It is open, Drew," she says.

❧

Marvin greets him, tail wagging, panting. He jumps on Drew and barks. How did he forget about his own dog? Or is it *her* dog now?

"Down, fella! Down, boy!"

"I hope you do not mind me giving your dog an old soup bone?"

Drew lifts his gaze to finally see her.

Fully clothed. Pretty. Wearing a simple white sundress, holding an open bottle of wine. "Welcome, Drew."

He hands her the pizza box, and she sets it on a wrought-iron patio table, artfully arranged with napkins and outdoor tableware. Nothing breakable, he hopes. She tells the dog to behave, and Marvin obeys with mind-boggling promptness. "Dinner is served," she smiles, placing a slice on each plate, blue eyes glancing flirtatiously up through tendrils of white-blond bangs.

Drew swallows and sits. His hand drifts toward the stem of his wineglass.

Her hand drifts toward his.

He stares at her.

She stares at him.

They try not to laugh.

A pot of geraniums. A basket full of begonias. Nodding peonies and daffodils. Blushing roses. Multicolored crepe myrtles and Rose of Sharon competing for notice. Everything in her garden seems to be in perpetual bloom. A redbud tree in Texas finishes blooming in March. It's June. The seasons have no expiration date in this woman's world.

Swiveling in his seat, he knocks over his wine glass. He looks down, mouth open, shocked.

"But it's impossible!"

Bluebonnets. Marigolds. Exotic orchids. Hibiscus, tropical and domestic. A riot of rainbow colors. Alyssum. Moss roses, daisies, and snow-white crocuses and pale violet hydrangea. Lilies, of all sorts. Orange trumpet vines and dripping honeysuckle. Whispering ferns and caladiums. Peach, apple and pear trees in full flower. Hello, bird of paradise.

He rises to his feet. "This is not happening. It can't—"

"Things bloom as long as I want them, too. Any season, any time." Her expression is inscrutable.

"No way—and don't say it's because you use Miracle Bloom."

"I have a green thumb, that's all," she shrugs, sipping her wine.

His spilled wine pools on the flagstones. Good thing it's unbreakable plastic. He reaches down to pick up the glass and her hand covers his. Her petal-soft fingers send a thrill through him that reaches all the way down to his toes.

"So green you can make plants grow out of season? Right."

"Sometimes. If you want something badly enough, things happen. What are you seeing here in my garden? What you want to see, or what is there? I've been wondering how long it would take for you to come see for yourself what you've been wanting for an awfully long time."

They stand up together, slowly.

Marvin puts his paws on the table and his nose quivers in the direction of the pizza box, then heads for the pizza on the closest plate. Drew feels frozen, unable to move.

The buttons on her thin dress hypnotize him for a second, and he locks his gaze on Kirsten's lips as they part to expose the tip of her tongue. His hands are trembling.

She leans forward and kisses him on each finger, then once on his right cheek, once on his left, after which she pulls back. She holds out her hand. He takes it. She leads him deeper into her garden.

The flowers also include Indian paintbrush, red-purple coneflowers, white Queen Anne's lace, Scottish and Mexican heather, larkspur, French lavender, and a few unknown species with starry space-alien protrusions and an intoxicating fragrance.

Rippling green grasses brush against their legs. Trees tower above them. Drew finds himself sighing.

"Are you, like, a botanist or some kind of expert? This isn't what they teach you at Home Depot."

She merely smiles. "So you like it?"

Stupid question. He shrugs and nods his head. "Are you kidding?"

They stop at an ornately carved wooden bench. "Sit."

He sits.

She stands in front of him.

"Sometimes we all need . . . cultivation. No?"

He glances back at the patio where Marvin is happily finishing their pizza. "Oh, wow. I'm so sorry Kirsten—it looks like Marvin just ate our dinner."

Leaning over him, she brushes her hands against the sides of his face. "That wasn't our dinner."

She kneels at his feet. Drew's eyes grow rounder. He could die now and be an almost happy man.

She stops.

Don't stop.

He reaches out impulsively to start unbuttoning her dress.

At the third button, a rosebud falls out of her cleavage. "Oh geez, wow. . . ."

At the fourth, a daisy.

He laughs softly.

At the fifth, a sprig of lilac.

At the sixth, honeysuckle. He remembers pulling the stamen out of honeysuckle and tasting its nectar for the first time when he was five. More, please. More.

At the seventh, a small gardenia.

He finds himself falling forward, dizzy with expectation.

It's dreamlike, hallucinogenic. He wonders if the wine had

been spiked, but doesn't even remember drinking it, anyway.

The stars are rising high in the sky and spinning. A full moon bursts behind a thread of silvery gray clouds.

A swallowtail butterfly flies alongside a Monarch.

Kirsten's dress pools at her feet.

He looks down at his goose-pimpled legs. Is there a monkey on that branch? Is that a bluebird, a crow, a cardinal, a finch? Is that a squirrel laughing and chattering? Is that a cougar sliding through the brush? Is that a wolf and a fox running past? Are those cats laughing at him? Is that Marvin with a little white dog?

He doesn't remember how his jeans got tangled in a bush. He doesn't know and he doesn't care. All he cares about is Kirsten and her kisses, now raining down on his chest and her hands. And how she smells like something he loves. Like wild irises.

Her tongue is a grape lollipop.

Her lips are pink cotton candy.

She is summer. She is winter. She is fall. She is spring.

Their legs are planted together. Their bodies are rooted in soil. They bloom. They reach up into the sky.

"Kiss me," she says, her fingers caressing and encouraging. Drew feels her hands diving into him deeper and deeper, down into the grass and into the mossy carpet of tiny yellow flowers.

She surrounds him. Their embrace grows more fevered and hushed. The water sprinklers come on. She must have them on a timer. Their joint laughter is like a waterfall. "Oh,

God!" he cries as he enters her, thinking he's the bee. But the stinging, almost painful joy of release has him wondering if she's the one determined to make honey. The sticky sweetness of nectar. The pollen of dreams. She won't let him stop. They roll over, and she looks down at him like a queen, her firm rosy nipples dripping sweet milk his tongue has to lick.

"No, you say, 'oh, Goddess,'" she corrects him, her wet hair fanning his heat with a thrilling, cool breeze.

"Oh, Goddess, *please*," he says.

She pulls the bud of a wild iris out of his ear.

THE BUTLER DID IT

༉ৡৄ

by Theresa Roland

Back in the sixties, when we bowed equally to Aquarius and equality, it was difficult to admit to coming from a household that had a butler. Harder still was confiding in your friends you'd lost your virginity to him.

But that's the way it was in those days. My father had finally been named an ambassador—recognized for his hefty contributions to the wrong party, of course—and the posting he received was to a tiny Caribbean country he labeled "strategically very important," but which my mother more accurately described as "a godforsaken place."

Whichever it was, it was sunny—if not downright arid—and the plan was for me to join them, with several friends, over the Easter break. Teenage girls love beaches, and the fact that it was going to be my first visit meant that we were going to have the fun of exploring the place together.

Unfortunately, the wintry tedium of March in New

England had driven me to accept a diabolical dare that affected these seemingly perfect plans. Mrs. Bradshaw, the headmistress of my boarding school, had banned all students from wearing any clothing "that makes a statement, either in words or symbols."

Everyone knew that she was anxious and upset because, on the weekends, some of us seniors had begun to sport T-shirts decorated with peace signs and the hairy mug of Che Guevara. What if some parent saw us and complained? If there was anything Mrs. Bradshaw dreaded it was "an incident," or, worse still, endangering alumnae contributions.

Well, there's more than one way to skin a cat, as they say. Egged on by my friends, I accepted their challenge to comply to the fullest extent with Mrs. Bradshaw's edict: I would wear no clothing that made a statement. That is, I would wear no clothing at all.

Naked, I strode into study hall, sat down on one of the hard wooden chairs and calmly opened my Latin text.

Mrs. Bradshaw decided not to suspend me only when my grandmother cannily offered to double her pledge for the new library building. But though my friends hailed me as a revolutionary heroine, their parents decided I was mad, bad and dangerous to know. Thus, when I boarded the flight in Miami, I found myself heading for the Caribbean all alone.

The ambassador's residence, a large, white Victorian building circled with porches and decorated with scrollwork, sat on a hillside overlooking the calm blue harbor. Not far from the swimming pool, in the back garden amidst a tangle of bougainvillea, was a shady gazebo. This quickly became my favorite spot, and it was where I sat poring over the book my friends had given me to compensate for their defection: the *Kama Sutra*.

I flipped the pages, enthralled with everything I read. The description of the eight different stages of oral intercourse were especially mesmerizing.

Breathing the heavy scent of frangipani, I let the words create a picture: a man coming slowly erect as I leaned over him, brushing the tip of his penis lightly with my fingers. The image aroused me, and I moved to the edge of the pool, letting one hand slide lightly across the top of the water as I practiced a touch as tentative as the brush of a butterfly's wing.

I found even that too exciting and rolled into the water, needing to cool down. Shivering, I floated on a raft under clouds that were like cutouts against an impossible azure brightness. A movement inside the house made me look toward the living-room window. A figure stood there: Martin, the butler my parents had hired on the last ambassador's recommendation.

Martin was young, thirty maybe, with the short, square build of the Welshman he was. Despite his stockiness, he had a presence that was probably due to the way he looked at you so intently before dropping his eyes in submission, his incredible dark lashes grazing his cheeks.

Martin shifted his position. Still at the window, he had now moved slightly to the side and was partly concealed by the long curtains with their glazed chintz flowers. As I drifted under the hot sun, I reached around and unhooked my bikini top, shrugging it off, feeling the cool lap of water against my breasts. When I finally climbed out, drops of water glistened on my breasts and I used my palms to stroke them dry before rubbing in the sun lotion. My fingers lingered on my nipples, pinching them lightly until they stood erect.

I was fantasizing that Martin was there watching, secretly wanting me, his head back, staring out at me under those heavy lashes. I stretched suggestively. Tilting my hips forward, I poured a stream of white lotion onto my belly and began massaging myself in large, circular motions, letting my hands slide down until they disappeared into my bikini bottom.

Though I could feel the high heat of afternoon burning my skin, what was even more scorching was the imagined heat of Martin's eyes.

Advice from the *Kama Sutra* on how to show a man you're interested: tremble and stammer when you address him.

The next morning I found Martin in the pantry, polishing silver wine coasters. I had put on a sheer, Indian cotton dress that barely covered my thighs and shamelessly revealed that I was braless. Trembling and stammering, I asked him if he ever went down into the town at night.

As he rubbed the cloth back and forth across the gleaming silver, he answered with a polite no. Since I was paying careful attention to his every syllable, it did seem to me that his trained courtesy seemed just the teeniest bit strained. Was there not a little trembling, a hint of a stammer, behind his aplomb?

The *Kama Sutra* says that a man will find it easy to seduce a woman if she puts a hand on his body and doesn't remove it even when he presses it between his thighs. I put my hand on his bare arm—his shirt was rolled up above the elbow—and boldly asked if he didn't get lonely. He did not press my hand between his thighs; at the same time, though, he made no move to withdraw.

I swam again that afternoon, repeating my earlier ritual of dispensing with my bikini top and letting my bare breasts bob above the water. This time, as I lay on the towel beside the pool, I slipped my hand between my legs and rubbed "the soft plump circle where the thigh joins the body."

The roses on the chintz drapes that covered the living room window shivered in the shadowy room.

The next afternoon was my mother's monthly tea. The Danish wife of the man who owned the island's largest hotel had come with her three small, blond children, who took generous handfuls of the little iced cakes Martin passed on a silver tray. One of the *Kama Sutra*'s less interesting suggestions had been, "Paying attention to a child, you could attract the notice of the loved one."

I had nothing to lose—so I lured one of the children over by offering him a tiny tart filled with custard and topped with a strawberry. Then I sat him on my lap, holding his sticky hands in mine, and began to recite the old nursery rhyme.

"This is the way the ladies ride, *ta da, ta da, ta da, ta da,*" bouncing him gently on my knee as I sang the refrain.

The little boy laughed, and I bounced him higher, deepening my voice and proclaiming, "This is the way the gentlemen ride, *a-room, a-room, a-room, a-room!*" He was shrieking with excitement and pleasure, and everyone was watching us.

Finally, I sent his small body high in the air with a vigorous, "and this is the way the huntsmen ride, *ka-boom, Ka-Boom, KA-BOOM!*"

When I looked to see if Martin was impressed, he was mopping up the tea the huntsman had spilled.

The next morning was a momentous one: my eighteenth birthday. Since my parents were to be away from lunchtime on, we celebrated early with a special treat—a pancake breakfast. I opened my gifts and made all the appropriate noises, but what I *really* wanted was not on any shopping list, and came without wrapping.

That afternoon, I swam in the pool and then lay on a towel beside it with my eyes closed, pretending that it was not my own fingers gently tweaking my nipples but Martin's square, strong hand.

My mother, ever thoughtful, had ordered a special dinner, which I ate alone at the dining room table as the overhead fan moved slowly around, forcing a slight breeze into the heavy air. When Martin poured a small dollop of wine in my glass, I put my hand over his and guided it back to fill the glass to the brim.

I was eighteen now, a child no longer.

When he brought in the cake with its candles, I held his eyes as I pressed my lips together to blow, giving out a long, steady exhalation that extinguished the flames and guaranteed I would get my wish.

Later, Martin was startled when I opened the door to his room wearing another of my Indian gauze dresses, this one as blue as lapis lazuli. I was tanned now, and the dress was thin enough to reveal quite clearly that I was wearing neither bra nor panties.

It was my birthday, and I was all alone, I mock-pouted. Couldn't we watch TV?

Poor Martin. He didn't know what to do and so he did nothing. I sat down next to him on a wicker couch with over-stuffed cushions. We stared at the screen with an intensity not merited by the picture, which, as a result of poor local reception, wiggled up and down and was streaked with snow. The *Kama Sutra* says, "A woman in love is ready for intercourse at any time of the day or night."

I rested my hand meaningfully on Martin's arm. I looked into his eyes, and when he lowered his wonderful lashes to hide from my gaze, I reached over to touch his lips lightly with my finger. He gave a sigh. I moved my hand to his leg.

Now, though, he was staring at me. Curiously, I thought—which seemed promising. But still he hung back.

Quickly, before he could protest or try to send me away, I rose and lowered myself onto his lap so that I sat, facing him. He wore a faint smile now, and he did not push me away.

"That little boy yesterday seemed to be having a good

time. I think it's my turn now." Martin was still watching me with an unreadable expression, wary but not unfriendly.

"This is the way the ladies ride," I began chanting, as I rubbed slowly back and forth on his lap until I felt a swelling hardness pressing between my legs. A corresponding warmth had started to spread throughout the center of my body; suddenly I was loose and dreamy, yet at the same time driven to continue the steady pressure that was having such an effect on us both.

"Don't." After all, a butler's life is as full of silly rules as a girls' boarding school. But I was sure he didn't mean it.

And I was right.

I was neither gentleman nor huntsman, I told him. So I rode him like a lady until he finally gathered the hem of my dress in his hands and lifted it over my head. He took my nipple in his mouth and sucked, at first softly, then harder. I moaned, and so did he, and, riding still, I slid back so that I could reach his zipper.

Suddenly I was awkward, not sure exactly how to do what I wanted to do. But Martin, ever the perfect butler, finally was willing to take charge of the situation. As he helped me free him from his trousers, his cock sprang forth erect and hard. I gasped: the *Kama Sutra* had hardly prepared me for its glory. I thought it was the most beautiful thing I had ever seen and told him so.

He laughed, then kissed me, and made me stand up so that he could explore me with a gentle, probing finger. When I sat down again, it was not his finger which went between my legs.

All that holiday, on the nights my parents were out, Martin and I watched TV.

When I went back to school, I was counting the days until graduation. Spending the summer with my normally boring parents had never seemed so appealing, and I managed to keep my secret even from my best friend. So imagine my dismay when I finally arrived on the island again—trunks and boxes following shortly thereafter—and a new butler greeted me blandly at the door.

Nonetheless, Martin had been indispensable.

SOUTHERN COMFORT

❧

by Laurel Gross

The young artist had come up north on the fifteenth of December, the coldest day of the year. Since he was used to Florida—where his skin wore only the soft sheen of sunlight and the delicate touch of water as he swam or waterskied the years away, gliding upon the backs of lakes in the landlocked district where he was born—it was especially hard for him.

New York City was all brick and asphalt, but he decided there was a certain cubist beauty in that. The problem was the wind that sneaked up on you suddenly, like a mugger. Boomeranging against the sides of buildings, it slid off the sheets of glass laced with metal—Mondrians without the color, he had thought—before striking him from behind.

He noticed with a certain modest pride that he was starting to develop, however slowly, a native's survival skills. A couple of times he had gone down into the shelter of a subway station and leaned against the side of the stairwell, in the same way ancient men must have sought solace in caves.

Today, though, weeks after his arrival by bus, it was simple hunger he needed to satisfy. The effort of making appointments and then meeting strangers to talk about elusive jobs had a way of whipping up his appetite. He knew he would find work eventually, but for the moment it was a matter of getting his portfolio seen—and no one paid you for that.

Luckily, in this city that never slept—even though its citizens needed to—there were places where one could nurse a cup of coffee for hours, or use the same tea bag over and over, refilling the mug with hot water.

While his mother's family had survived their lean years on the alligator tail, snake meat, birds' eggs and swamp cabbage they had managed to forage in the Everglades, here there seemed to be a restaurant on every corner. Many of them were called coffee shops, though they seemed to serve almost everything you could think of.

Nothing focuses the mind like the prospect of starvation, his mother had always said. Pausing before the door to the nearest coffee shop, he took a deep breath and went inside, angling himself up on a tall stool surrounded by empty ones.

It seemed quiet. Then, in the twinkling of an eye, the whole place suddenly filled. Not an empty seat anywhere. If it had been an Edward Hopper a moment before, now it was Brueghel. There were people standing behind him three deep, waving their arms wildly.

Every time he tried to get the attention of the waitress, she seemed to float past him. Back home, he was considered a catch and not likely to be ignored. But, here, the waitress always seemed to be looking at someone else. If he had been a fellow of a different temper, the type to bruise easily, the kind quick to pick fights in bars and pool halls, he might have been convinced that she was—quite deliberately—avoiding him. Except for the fact that he took up a seat, and a volume of air, he might as well have been invisible.

Suddenly he noticed the slender young woman sitting next to him. She had materialized on the cushioned pillar to his right as if by magic. And she seemed already to be well in progress nursing a tall glass of water without ice—taking the tiniest sips through a straw. He had to admire the way this exotic bird of a girl looked so entirely comfortable perched on her metal stand. A peacock-blue coat was neatly balanced on her lap and seemed to hang from the balance of her body like plumage.

He wondered why he—who possessed such a good eye for even the tiniest sliver of detail, always alert to his surroundings—had only this instant become aware of her existence. He supposed that, perhaps, the fact of her silence and supreme stillness might account for such a sin of omission. But it was an indisputable fact that she was of that rare type of beauty frequently seen painted or photographed while almost never encountered in real life.

She was, in short, difficult to miss.

Her long legs, the tops of which were covered by the smallest awning of a skirt, dangled gracefully from the tall stool. On the plate in front of her was a slice of tomato buoyed up on a single large frond of lettuce. As yet, it had not been touched. A clump of parsley, too large to be mere garnish, sat on top of the tomato like a feathery hat.

"You have to shout," she said.

"Excuse me?"

"You have to speak up." She sliced off the tip of the lettuce leaf. "Otherwise you'll starve here."

He found it hard to believe that such a delicate-seeming creature could ever be so assertive.

"This is New York," she said. "You can't be shy."

He felt his face getting red. Mama had always teased him because, as a child, he had had a tendency to blush whenever he felt something intensely. Now, in the midst of this cruel New York winter, he felt hot. Almost steamy. Downright southern-summer steamy.

"You should know what you want before you sit down. So when you come in you don't even need to look at the menu."

He tried to collect his wits, to act as if he belonged here— the way he belonged, say, in the Fakahatchee. But he felt he was moving stiffly. Though he hadn't eaten much for days, all of a sudden his pants felt tight.

"Forget the menu?" he said.

"Yeah." The timid little person that he'd imagined her to be was definitely a figment of his imagination. In its place was a real New Yorker. With a real New York voice, the kind that had all the edges sawed off and the teeth of the saw left behind in the wood.

"Okay," he said. "What's good?"

She crossed, then recrossed, those long gorgeous legs. They were booted to the knee, and she made the most of the squishy sound of the expensive black leather as she slid them against each other. Either that, or his hearing, had—suddenly—become as acute as a dog's.

"How would I know?" she replied. She sliced off another minute forkful of lettuce. "You see what I eat. Not much variety."

She smiled for the first time. It felt, to him, like an invitation. Because she didn't clam up. Or stop there. "I never eat anything else."

"Never?"

"Well, on rare occasions. A holiday, or something."

Or something? He was intrigued now. He had seen the movie *Tom Jones*. His favorite scene was the one where the hero and the heroine seduce each other while working their way through an elaborate feast: sucking on bones, smacking their lips and such, all the while staring into each other's eyes from opposite ends of a long table.

He watched the girl cut a tiny edge off the tomato, then chew it luxuriantly, as if it were steak.

Tom Jones this was not.

Still, seeing her eat made him hungrier—and not just for food. "What's that?" he said, pointing to a plate that arrived like a special delivery in front of the man on his other side. The fellow was a late arrival who had just taken the place of someone else who had already finished and who had, in fact, also come in after him.

"Bagel." She smiled again. "It's called a bagel."

"I've heard of them. But what's that on it?"

"Cream cheese. Though you could have butter, if you want."

"Which do you prefer?"

"Me?" She laughed. "Do I look like I eat bagels?" She ventured another infinitesimal slice off the tomato, which still had a way to go. "Not even on Christmas."

"I wasn't sure," he said. "I didn't know."

"Anyway, it's a New York thing," she explained.

"Okay," he said. "Bagel!"

The waitress stopped, as if he had slammed on her brakes. She was looking at him as if he had only just now come in, taking the place of whomever else had been on the stool. She took out her pad and smiled. "With what?"

"Cream cheese." He was feeling good about this. And he was going to get fed.

"Kind?" she said.

Huh?

She tapped her pen on the pad. "What kind of bagel?"

"Oh. What kinds do you have?"

One of her arched eyebrows seemed to straighten out into a line of frustration. You could tell she didn't like this part of the job. It required her to slow down, while maybe somebody was snatching up her tips. Her recitation sounded so much like a bored train conductor's, you might have thought she was announcing a series of commuter destinations: "Plain, poppy seed, sesame seed, cinnamon-raisin, pumpernickel, onion."

"Plain."

You could see she was darn fed up to be led on so. What else would a white boy with a southern accent order, her glance seemed to say.

She swiveled her hips, reversing herself, so that now her right side was lower than the left. "Toasted?"

He looked at the girl, then at the waitress. He felt very sure of himself. Confidently, he told her, "Toasted."

It was the waitress's exit cue. She was gone in a flash. The girl leaned over, allowing her arm to graze the counter. She raised both hands and clapped like a child. "That wasn't so hard, was it?" she said.

There was no doubt in his mind that she was teasing him somehow. But it was being done nicely, and he had to admit it felt pretty good. He decided that he liked being played with—at least by her. He wouldn't even mind being laughed at, he decided—that is, if she'd a mind to.

Who'd have believed it?

She looked at him curiously.

"I feel like a virgin," he said. "Who has, you know, just done 'it.'"

"You eat slowly," he said.

He had wolfed down most of his bagel in a few bites. She was still working her way through the lettuce, tomato and parsley. He had never seen anyone make so much of so little.

Perhaps some serious comment was coming, because she

put down her knife and fork, and looked thoughtful. Either she couldn't digest and talk at the same time, or what she was going to say to him required her full attention.

"I don't eat often or a lot, so I have to make it last." She had lowered her head slightly but was still looking at him, her eyes steady in their gaze. It seemed to him that there was suddenly a new, more vulnerable person there, and that that new person was telling him something important.

Something, perhaps politeness—but also respect—kept him from responding. He just waited for her to form some more words with those pretty little lips of hers. Tomato-red they are, he thought. Not sickly pink like the ones you saw in the supermarkets, but the crimson of the awesomely scented, straight-from-the-vine tomatoes that leaked delicious warm juice down your chin.

"You have to do it slowly. Make it last. The best things are done slowly," she said. "It's like with dance. You practice years and years, a whole lifetime, to get just twenty seconds of perfection."

He couldn't believe his luck. She had actually opened up a door that he might now waltz right through. "Didn't Martha Graham say that?"

He wanted to sound as nonchalant as possible, but his excitement was such that he thought he heard his voice actually quaver. Had she noticed?

For the first time he well and truly saw the eyes of the girl on the stool: they seemed to grow larger and larger. They were dark, almost black, but if you looked at them—really looked—the pupils were lighter, and, even in this unbecoming glare, they were streaked with glimmers of gold.

More than once, while working, he had knocked over a bottle of drawing ink, and now her eyes reminded him of those ever-widening stains, ink sprawling across paper with the speed of a flash flood. He had heard of people who, having misjudged the depth and velocity of fast-cresting flood water, had navigated their cars along a stretch of mud-layered road, only to drown just a few yards from where they'd felt safe. And, for a moment, he was afraid that her eyes might be just as deep and deceptive.

What if he was about to get into something from which he might not know when to escape? His mama often said that, some mistakes in life, you could get trapped in them forever.

He briefly wondered if his mother's mother had passed along that same warning to her. After all, one marriage and eleven children later, she would have known what she was talking about.

The girl's voice now woke him up from his reverie. "How did you know that?" Her smile showed teeth now. Perhaps she had grown more comfortable in his presence, because her whole body was seeming to sway toward his. "About Martha Graham."

He felt another flush of heat spread across his face. "An art teacher of mine mentioned it once. He liked to say one art wasn't so different from another. They all contribute to each other. At least the best art does, of course. That's what he told us."

"And did he say any more on the subject?"

"Just that some famous artist—I can't remember his name—was asked how long it took him to paint a single picture. Lots of people think it's a matter of hours, or days, or months, you see. So this artist, who was asked the same stupid question all the time, answered, 'It takes a lifetime.'"

"The same way you get to Carnegie Hall," she said.

"The same way you get anywhere worth getting to," he said. But then he felt sad. And, suddenly, anxious.

"What's the matter?" she asked.

"Those twenty seconds of perfection—if they were possible, all that work might be worth it. But," he told her as he pushed his empty plate away, "nothing's perfect."

"Well, we must try," she said. "We must give the iilusion. And to do that, to achieve that, you know, we must be very, very good."

"Perfect," he said.

"Near as."

Even before she had quoted Martha Graham, he knew his companion was a dancer. He just knew it, and he couldn't have explained it, because words weren't his thing at all. But, with a body and a spirit and a face like hers, what else could she be?

She stuck her fork into a piece of lettuce, into which she then placed the last of the slowly disappearing tomato. Then she looked him in the eyes. "Would you like me to show you the town?" she asked.

It was not necessary for him to speak at all. She understood. "Good. But, first, I have to finish this," she said.

She ate the rest of her salad serenely. He said nothing, only watched her happily.

❦

He saw nothing of "the town," and it didn't matter. He could visit all of those places himself one day. Or never. Most New Yorkers, he knew, whether native-born or hailing from the great beyond, had never seen half of them.

What he did see was the inside of a high-rise apartment, on the thirtieth floor of a white-brick building near Lincoln Center. The living room into which she ushered him seemed to be the very definition of calm. Zen-like and minimal, with little if anything personal about it.

Like a stage, he thought. A place of possibility. Uncluttered. But also unanchored. As if the ballerina could, with little trouble, transplant herself somewhere else. He relaxed.

It was so soothing, this stillness.

In truth, he was no more a child of the south than he was a Parisian. He could be anybody. He could do anything. The entire room, and his body, and hers, within it, seemed charged with possibility. An electric sensation coursed through him. As if he'd put his finger in an outlet and found it a pleasant experience. An out-of-body, otherworldly experience.

He felt all of a sudden as if he could live many lives. That he had whatever heart and passion it might take. He sensed that he might have the ability to reinvent himself many times—perhaps an infinite number of times.

"Come," she said. She took him by the hand. Usually he was the one to lead, but this time he followed.

He did not care where she took him, or what she did with him. As long as it did not require words or thought. Those things had been released from his mind. He felt just-born. Everything seemed fresh, larger than he remembered, and thrilling.

Her bedroom was large and white, nothing but a featherbed, sheets and pillows. All cloud. The carpet melted into his feet.

"Take your shoes off," she said.

He stood there, shoeless, like the country boy he was. Toes feeling the blades of grass under him. The fresh scent of the grass.

"Take off your shirt," she said.

He couldn't have remembered how it came off; even seconds later, the memory of it was already gone. There was only the moment. This moment, and no other. She slid her hand against his chest. Her touch was almost as soft as a child's.

But more amazing still was the response her caress elicited from him. This feeling of vulnerability, yet of being safe, in good hands. The best hands. He stood like a small boy and waited for her next request, not wanting the moment or the sensations to end.

She grazed him gently with her cheeks, and lips. Then stood back as though inspecting a painting in a gallery, and looked, and looked. It was as if the intensity of all the eyes that had ever watched her perform onstage somehow had been stored up in her and, now, released, was concentrated on him.

Finally, she came close, and leaned her head against his chest.

"You're beautiful," she said.

He looked at her, wondering what she'd say or do next. It was indescribably wonderful.

"Lie down," she said.

She straddled his legs, then pulled off his pants.

"Is this all right?" she asked.

She caressed his legs, then took him into her hands.

Her fingers skied first down one side and then another, and began swirling all around him in a pattern that was always changing. None of that pumping, strictly up-and-down motion, like the girls back home, or even the more sophisticated ones whom he had encountered in Miami or New Orleans.

She was so adept at these maneuverings that, if he hadn't known she was a dancer, he most certainly would have taken her for a member of that Other Profession, the one your mother and the army cautioned you about.

Then, just when he thought his head and maybe entire body would implode from pleasure, she took him in her mouth.

"It's your turn," he said. They had been napping, giving him a bit of time to regain his strength.

He had said, "I don't know why you wanted me to go off like that, so soon."

She had turned her head and smiled. "I think you can handle it. And, anyway, I'm in no hurry."

So he painted her face with kisses, then lay still beside her.

She stood up now, and after stretching out her limbs in a glorious display of agility, tilted her head to one side. He had once had a cat who had looked at him precisely that way. "Are you coming, or not?" she—the cat—would seem to be asking.

Her own body was perfect. Her breasts were small and round, her belly a gentle swell. Of course her calves were rock-hard, as tight as stone, and he now massaged them until the bulges under the skin loosened and she became soft again.

Her feet, callused and tough, reminded him of orphans desperately in need of some loving.

Partnering her in this part of their dance, he lifted her off her scarred but beautiful feet and carried her to the bed. Then he proceeded to rub those troubled soles. She writhed and moaned with pleasure.

"All I do is dance," she said. "My feet bleed like Christ's."

"Why do you do it?"

She propped herself up on her elbow, like some pale pink

odalisque against the fresh whiteness of the room. "Why do you draw?"

His answer was his silence. He knew he couldn't answer that any more than she could. It was just something he did, had always done. And he loved it. He just couldn't stand it if he didn't have something to draw.

"Do you hurt?" she said. "I mean, are you in pain all the time when you draw?"

"I almost never ache from that," he said. "I only feel bad when I can't get the effect I want."

"Dedication is the only thing that works. Dedication, and discipline," she added. "And no matter what happens . . . you don't give up."

"It's a pretty farfetched idea, making a living as an artist," he said. That morning he had visited an ad agency and, for the umpteenth time, had tried to appear interested in coming up with visual concepts for its clients.

"Dancers don't generally have any better luck. And they haven't got time for anything else, so it's hard to make money if you're not in a company. But even the most famous companies are more like cults than any paying profession. Our ballet master doesn't even want us to date. Much less marry. He says you can't do both. You know, have a relationship. And dance. Impossible."

"Do you think that's true?"

"I don't think about it," she said.

He could see that her eyes, suddenly, were moist. He didn't know if it was because of her feet—the effect his deep massage was having on their delicate and overused tissue—or because of the sensitive subject that neither of them had meant to broach.

"All I do is dance," she said. "It's all I've ever done, so I must keep doing it."

❧❧

After a suitable interval, he lay beside her and opened her legs. Her eyes were dry now, but she was very wet below. Her body bent upward into an arch, then relaxed flat against the sheets. He imagined her crying like the wail of the wind that had been rushing past his ears these weeks, but this was different—this would be a beautiful sound.

Why did he feel that his destiny lay here between her legs?

The exquisite pain of loving, and maybe losing—he felt he had to try it once.

He had made love to women, had had sex with many more, but he had never felt like this. He put his head between her long legs and dug his lips deep into the crevice where they joined her body. She quivered as strings do when the music is plucked from them.

Remembering when she had explained why the "best things" must be done slowly—"I have to make it last," she'd said—he decided to switch gears. He put a finger inside her, feeling his way inside until he detected the hidden pad of flesh located under the roof of her womb, in that part of the cavern that lay just under the tip of her triangle.

And, touching it, he made her wail—soft and low and steady, so that he felt it echo in his very bones.

꘏

And then she opened to him wholly, and asked him to come into her. This happened so naturally it required no effort.

But once inside, he felt like he was drowning. She leaned over to one side, taking him with her. And, then, he found his pace and rhythm again. It was a strange sort of music this time. But each of them seemed to know the melody—and the harmony.

And when it was nearly over, and they lay entwined, he found his mind, independent of his body, wondering how this would end.

All things ended, he had been taught, in their season. But what was this? An ending? Or a beginning?

He was not prepared to be grasping or needy. He wasn't the type. He would go away when she showed him the slightest sign. All he knew was that, in these few incredible hours, he had lost nothing.

And gained everything.

He was so far ahead of where he'd been when he had ducked into that coffee shop to get fed and away from the December cold, that he told himself whatever happened from here on in would be . . . all right.

But he knew he was fooling himself.

He put his hand behind her neck to ease out any residue

of tension, but he was surprised to discover that her muscles and skin now were soft and yielding.

She curled over and leaned her head on his chest. "Do you want to see me dance?" she said. "I've got some tickets you can have."

"I've already seen you dance."

"My best work?" she said, and reached out to touch his cheek gently.

He smiled. "A command performance."

MAMA SAID

❧

by Maura Anne Wahl

When my second year of high school ended for the summer, I was bored right away. Ida and Charlotte and Geraldine were still exclaiming over their joy at being out of old Miss Carter's sophomore English class and away from her infernal Shakespeare and Wordsworth and compositions. But me, I missed old Miss Carter and Julius Caesar. I missed wandering lonely as a cloud.

Instead, I stood in front of the faded mirror on Grammy's old bureau and fooled with my hair. Me and Geraldine painted our eyes and mouths into Mary Pickford and Clara Bow, stealing a lipstick here and cream rouge there, using up Mama's powder. After we were beautiful, we'd make Billie sit down on the bed and do her face, too.

Grammy caught a glimpse of us, sighed, shook her head and asked us if we wanted to look like those harlots downtown. In the shade at the bottom of the backyard, drinking sweet tea and smoking cigarettes in secret, Geraldine and I speculated about what life was like for the downtown girls who wore nice clothes and worked in big buildings and ate their lunch in restaurants, and what Grammy had against them.

They seemed only a step away from our ideals—the beautiful, glamorous Hollywood girls who had money and power of their own, and a line of handsome men to choose from—a different fellow for every gorgeous ensemble. Such men would treat their women like queens, arrive in big cars to escort them to fancy parties and nightclubs, kiss their hands hello and good-bye, and hold their slender bodies like rare flowers while they glided them across the dance floor.

Eventually the Hollywood girl would choose the king among these suitors, the one who loved her the most passionately and understood her the best. They would marry in a headline-making ceremony in a cathedral, a line of little girls in pink satin dresses scattering rose petals for them to walk on as they exited into the blue-skied morning, where thousands waited for them, throwing rice, bearing gifts, weeping with joy, waving them into a waiting horse-drawn carriage that bore them down to the pier where they would board a gleaming white ocean liner bound for the Orient and then the South Pacific.

The downtown girls' stories always followed a similar path. Not so grand, but just as dreamy in their own way. There was nothing dirty or unpleasant or hard about marriage, not as we saw it: the marriages around us, and the ones we planned on having ourselves, had nothing in common. I wanted what I dreamed about and it was more real than real life to me, and more so than ever on those hot summer days.

Coming out of the Odeon into the blinding afternoon sun, all soaked in beauty and love's young dream, having just watched Valentino be so gorgeous we could hardly stand it, Ida and I ran into three older boys on the sidewalk. One of them, Floyd, was a friend of Ida's big sister, while the other two were his buddies. They wanted to treat us to Cokes at Skillern's. Ida and I exchanged looks, her's saying she wasn't so sure, mine saying "let's." And since I always have my way, a few minutes later we were all in a red vinyl booth at the back, Ida on one side between Floyd and Randall, and me on the other with Roy Thornton, who had maneuvered himself into that spot as we filed in. I had seen Roy around school, but he was older than me and we'd never spoken. I hadn't known he even knew I was alive. He was a very good-looking boy: tall, with dark eyes and hair combed back like one of those screen lovers I couldn't get enough of.

While Ida listened to Floyd and Randall joke back and forth about her sister, Roy leaned close to me and asked me where I lived, and did I know so-and-so, and how had I liked the movie. I was pleased by his attention and answered his questions, slipping in a wisecrack or two. I even teased him a little, feeling quite the vamp because a handsome fellow like him seemed so taken with me. Soon he had me pressed back into the corner of the booth, and I noticed his buddies watching us and smiling. Ida, on the other hand, was looking a little sore.

With everyone listening, Roy asked me then if I wanted to go for a ride with him sometime. I hadn't gone on any real dates before, so I didn't answer right away. I wondered what Mama would say. Probably that she'd have to meet him first. Then Randall piped up, "She looks like she'd like to go for a ride."

"Yeah," agreed Floyd, "a nice long one."

"How about it, honey," said Roy, "you feel like going on a nice long ride with me? I guarantee you'd enjoy it."

Ida looked grim. She was jealous, I guessed.

"Sure," I said, ignoring her baleful stare. "Sounds like fun."

All three boys started laughing like I'd made the best joke in the world.

On the way home, Ida said she had heard that Roy was running around with Eugene Ferris, who'd already been in jail once for stealing a car, and that she knew for a fact Roy had quit school just before the end of the year. I said, in a voice filled with wide experience of the world, that didn't everybody quit school sometime and who did we know who hadn't stolen a car or been chased through the Bogs by the cops. She said she didn't know about me, but, as far as she was concerned, she wouldn't go out with a boy like Roy Thornton because he drank hooch and talked dirty and was conceited and meant trouble and I ought to know better.

She said I knew just as well as she did all about what he'd done to Dorothy Dalton. I chose to reply to this by saying wasn't his hair lovely the way he'd slicked it back like Valentino's? She snorted and gave up trying to talk me out of it, and just said it was corny for anyone except Valentino to do that to his hair, and that Roy Thornton wouldn't be caught dead watching a Valentino picture.

"Neither would Valentino, I bet. He just lives it," I said. Ida said Mama would skin me and I said that no, she wouldn't—at least not today. What she didn't know wouldn't hurt her. Mama wasn't going to stand in the way of me getting my hand kissed or finally being treated like the lady she was always telling me I was.

Once home, I locked myself in the bathroom and did myself over inch by inch. I let Billie in to pee, and she sat there on the commode doing her business and asked me what I was up to because I'd scrubbed myself red and plucked my eyebrows and styled my hair a dozen different ways. I said I was going out to a movie with a boy after supper.

"A *boy*," she said, as if that was a disappointment. She was eleven, and she hated boys.

"Yes, a boy," I said. "Now get out of here and let me have some privacy."

Mama came home from work, and I heard Billie tell her that I had a date and was all worked up about it. A minute later Mama tapped on the bathroom door and said she heard I had a date and to come and tell her about it when I was done. I did and she asked me with what boy and where did he live and who were his parents and what would we do on this date. I made up what I didn't know for sure, but still she had more to say. She paused, though, and I knew what she was going to talk about next. We'd had this kind of talk before, not because I was going on a date, but because I was growing up.

"Just remember men and women are different, Bonnie," she said.

"I know that, Mama," I said.

"You don't touch a boy," she told me. "You don't touch anyone until you're planning on getting married."

"I know all that."

"Don't you laugh. You listen to me. Men get ideas in the blink of an eye. You touch a man and he figures you're fast."

I cleared my throat to cover up a snicker. Sometimes she was so naïve.

"If you kiss a boy, and you're touching him somewhere on his body at the same time, he's going to take advantage—but you're not to let him! You understand me?" and then she stood up and brushed off her skirt, which meant she had a thousand other things to see to right then.

❧

At seven, Roy came to the door and shook hands with Uncle Sam and Uncle Willie and Buster, who, for a change, showed some interest in my doings, although not the good kind of interest. When we went out to Roy's old Model-T touring car with the canvas roof rotted away, they all followed us onto the porch and watched us drive off. Buster stood behind the uncles with his arms folded across his chest. He seemed to know something about Roy he didn't like, and, if that was so, it was just a matter of time before everyone else in the family would know it too.

As he drove, Roy said the car belonged to a friend and that he himself planned to put money down on a car of his own with his first check from the boiler works. Plus, he already had $75 in the bank from doing odd jobs. Then he said I was the prettiest girl he'd ever seen, and stopped the car right there in the middle of the road to pull me close and kiss me hard and press the breath out of me. Lord, I still remember what that kiss did to me. Every nerve in my body stood up and cheered. Parts of me I never even knew I had tingled. I got hot all over, and Roy pressed his leg up against me.

Then a car came behind us and honked, and Roy put the Ford back into gear and we drove to the Grand on Eagle Ford and saw *Ben Hur*. Ramon Novarro was half naked for most of it and the handsomest thing ever seen on a movie screen. During the show, Roy slid his arm around my shoulders and squeezed me now and then. Afterward we strolled down a few blocks, his arm around my waist and hand resting on my hip, and he gave me a Camel and lit it for me. I resolved to take up full-time smoking.

The night air was soft and warm and private, and the stars were clear white, like little flames above the streetlights and store windows. I was grown up and gorgeous and liked how near Roy was and how tall he was and how he hung on my words even though all I had to talk about was my family and school and the movies. When he brought me home, we sat in the dark car out front and kissed harder and longer than before without stopping once. He slid his hands over my legs and behind and stomach and cupped a hand under my left breast for a moment. He pulled my hand over along his thigh and rested it between his legs. Something poked against his trousers and jumped at my touch. He left my hand there and slid his between my legs again.

I tingled again, and wanted more. While we were kissing and feeling each other, though, I could sense Mama lying in bed awake waiting for me to come in, and I got more and more afraid she'd come charging out there any second, and then would I be in hot water.

It was only fear of her wrath that made me pull myself out of Roy's arms. I said goodnight regretfully, leaving behind those kisses that numbed my brain and lit my body on fire. I went inside as quiet as I could and slipped under the sheet next to Billie. Being a kid, she was already asleep, so I could lie there in the dark dreaming as long as I wanted. All I could see was his face, and all I could feel were his hands and lips and that slow fire that had been burning inside me.

By the next day, Mama had learned the truth about Roy and his reform school days and his uncle's bootlegging and how he'd been running wild for years. She said she knew full well what kind of boy he was and so must I, and no good could come of it. She told me I was better than him and that there was no way she would allow me to throw myself away on such a common, ill-behaved creature whose companions and relations alike weren't worth the fleas on any old dog.

"Do you understand me, young lady?" she said.

"Yes, ma'am," I said. And I did understand how she felt, and so that afternoon when I left the house to meet Roy instead of going to Rosa's like I'd said I was going to, I felt a sadness like cold spring water shoot through me and then trickle slowly away. It wasn't there, though, when I met Roy at our agreed-upon corner and climbed into the Ford's sprung front seat.

Although only the day before I had had no time to spare on boys, it suddenly seemed that I had gone too long without something completely essential. Much like the times when I would pine for a piece of chocolate and cry into my pillow because I had neither the chocolate itself nor the nickel to buy some, now all I wanted was to be with Roy and dance close to him under a starry sky.

That afternoon, after riding around for two hours or more and talking, Roy finally pulled into an old lane, where tree branches arched over the dirt road from both sides. It was kind of pretty there, and I felt happy that he had brought me and was talking to me and listening to what I said. He stopped the engine and drew out a pint jar from under the seat. After he'd screwed off the lid and drunk some, he offered it to me. I swallowed a gulp of what smelled like gasoline and then burned its way down from my mouth into my stomach.

Mama said no lady touched hard liquor. She sometimes allowed us half glasses of beer when the uncles would gather at our house for parties, and I had been sneaking swallows of wine for years. As Roy watched me take that first swallow, he laughed at the look on my face and called me a kid. I was stung. I took a second drink and kept my face still this time.

"That's my girl," he said, and took another mouthful before tapping us both a Camel out of his pack. While he held a match to my cigarette, the hooch buzzed in my ears and eyes and mixed with the light and dark shadows swapping over our heads. With the taste of alcohol and smoke in our mouths, we kissed long and deep, his arm tightening around me as our breathing got louder. We broke apart and washed down the rest of our cigarettes with another swallow. Then, without speaking, we fell into kissing again and Roy undid the round pearly buttons on my red-print dress and slid a hand all over my breasts before settling on the right nipple which he worked softly between his fingers.

"Nice little titties," he said approvingly. "Small, but real nice." With the first touch of his hand on my skin, I gasped and my eyes shut and my head went light, it felt so fine.

He stopped and drew away from me then, taking another pull from the jar before he asked almost shyly, "You like riding with me?"

I straightened myself out and buttoned up my dress and said I did. I thought of teasing him by saying Mama had warned me about boys like him, but if he took it wrong I knew he'd have me home like a shot and that would be the last I'd see of him. And I liked him a lot. Most of all, I wanted him to like me back.

"I sure do like you, Roy," I said. I felt like a fool telling him, but there it was. He said he liked me too and put his hands on my breasts again and stroked the nipples, poking up hard, through my dress top and brassiere. I felt fit to burst, but I had something I wanted to say first. "I heard about you and Dorothy Dalton," I blurted out.

"Did you?" Roy said, not missing a beat, rolling my nipples between his fingers.

I put a hand on his wrist to make him quit, even though I didn't honestly want him to stop. "Are you going to ruin me?"

"Ruin you?" he said, and shook off my hand and started opening my dress again, slower this time, playing with the buttons. "How can I ruin you if we're going to get married?"

"Married!" I said. I was shocked. But not. Maybe this was how you did it, being the part left out of my dreams.

As long as we were planning on getting married, Roy said, it was okay to go ahead and do it all we wanted. What did I say, he wanted to know. Were we engaged? Because he was all for it.

"I have to think about it for a little while," I said, my heart pounding, wondering maybe if a whole plan for my life hadn't suddenly just opened up before me.

"You think all you want. But we should have a few more drinks while you do," Roy said, and he handed me the jar first. When he took it back from me, he had another swallow himself, put the lid back on, and sat looking at me, not touching me, just looking and smiling. And not a smart-aleck grin like I'd seen him shoot his friends, but a real sweet smile, a happy one.

"You really are the prettiest girl I've ever seen," he said. "I wasn't just saying that yesterday. You got the prettiest face, like a movie star's." He put out a finger and poked a curl back from my face, his touch light as a breeze. "Your eyes are the same blue as cornflowers. I never saw eyes like yours before."

He was so sweet with what he was saying I nearly cried. I knew I was okay-looking, but it meant something big when it came from a swell young man like Roy and was not just something Mama told me. He handed me the jar again, and said "Here's to us!" when he took his own drink.

I thought things over. The idea was so wild, so unplanned, but also romantic and right. I said yes. He leaned over to me then, and we kissed for a long time. His hands went inside my dress. He had most of my buttons open again.

"But I have to tell Mama first. *You* have to tell her," I said. She was going to take some convincing. He sat back again and caught my hands up and looked me calmly in the eye.

"This ain't between me and your mama," he said, and he lifted my hands to his mouth and kissed the palms. "This is between us. We don't have to get anyone's permission to do what we want. And I know you want to, just like I do. Don't you?" He let go of one of my wrists to stroke me between the legs. It felt so good I moaned, and he smiled. "See?" he said. "All that will take care of itself."

"I've never done this before," I said, all thoughts of Mama and marriage slipping out of my mind.

"I know, but don't you worry about that," Roy said. "I'll show you how." He slipped his hand inside my panties and pushed them down to my knees. He gently pushed me down on the seat and stroked me with his hand and put his mouth down to a nipple and began to suck. I wanted to touch his skin and began to fumble open his shirt buttons. I slipped my hands onto his bare chest and down to his belly. His skin was so smooth, smoother than I would have ever thought. He helped me loosen his belt—I heard the buckle clink—and, when his pants were open, took my hand again and slid it down to where it touched his thing, standing stiff and hot inside his drawers.

I was going too far, too far, I knew it, and didn't care. It came into my head then that this was how girls got in trouble. I hadn't understood before. But now it was too late: I was crazy to know it all and see what Roy was going to do with that thing of his. He called me honey and sweetheart and kissed me hard on the lips for a long, long time, holding my hand there on his thing and moving it up and down.

It wasn't until we'd climbed over into the big backseat that he saw me full naked. He stopped dead, like he'd been poleaxed. At the same time, the birds stopped singing and the breeze dropped to nothing.

He just stared at me.

My heart stopped, just like the breeze. What was wrong? We weren't going to be married? No more of this fooling around? I'd just decided to give myself over to him body and soul, and now he was changing his mind. I quick grabbed his arm and said, "Roy, sweetie?"

"I knew you had little titties. But I didn't realize you were so . . . well, small, all over," he said. He sat back against the seat.

"That doesn't matter."

"Well, it does. How old are you, anyway?"

"I got hair there," I said. "I can't help being small. I was born that way." And I felt panicky, because, all of a sudden, he wasn't going to ruin me anymore.

"Now, come on, hey," he said. "Don't carry on. Everything's all right. You don't have to cry." I just knew he was changing his mind about me. Tears had welled up in my eyes.

"Why'd you bring me out here, and why'd you say we'd get married," I said, "if you were going to change your mind all of a sudden?"

"Hey."

"Can't we just try it?" I put my arms around his neck, pressed myself against his warm skin, and cried on him. He put his arms around me too and pulled me close. Pretty soon he laid me down on my back on the seat and lowered himself onto me, holding his thing in his hand and pushing it around here and there to get it in. In a while, he found the spot and pushed in—and I gasped because it was so tight and I felt full to bursting. After he got it in me good, he pushed it up still higher into me, and I started to feel little waves of sensation that surprised me.

Then he pulled it out a little and then up again, and I

began to see how it worked. Things I couldn't describe were sparking inside me when, all of a sudden, he gave a groan and a few gasps and bucked hard up into me. Then he got all still and flopped over beside me, with his eyes closed and his breath coming hard through his mouth. I kept on moving, but he stopped me.

"What?" I said. "Aren't I doing it right or something?"

"Hell, yes, you're doing it right, but that was it. I'm done. I gotta catch my breath."

"Done? What do you mean, done?"

"Just for right now, honey," he said.

"Huh," I said. "Well, okay."

We lay together on the Ford's big backseat, looking up at the treetops, and I listened to my heart slow down and the summer birdsongs come back into hearing. I slid my arm around Roy's neck and kissed his cheek a hundred times. I felt good, and the breeze moving over my skin was pleasing.

When Roy left me at the corner at twilight, I watched him go and blew him kisses until he had driven out of sight. We'd done it twice more, each time longer than before, and I was sore between my legs, and my lips were swollen and scraped and hot. I was sweaty and in need of a bath, though I knew no amount of water would alter how I'd changed since morning.

Riding back beside Roy, I had felt full of love and the future, but, walking alone now along the dry dirt roadside, a small dark corner in my heart opened suddenly to my full view and I felt a million miles from everything familiar: home, school, girlfriends, and, most of all, myself. Nothing would ever be the same, and, for a long sad minute, I missed that old way with all my heart.

But there was no going back. I was crazy in love.

A TASTE OF REBECCA

❧

by Susan St. Aubin

Charlotte followed Evelyn everywhere. After they worked together all day on their puff pastry or soufflés at the College of Culinary Arts, Charlotte would clatter down the stairs behind Evelyn, asking endless questions about class, about cooking and recipes, about Evelyn's boyfriend. Evelyn began to fantasize murder: poison in Charlotte's crème brûlée, or a well-placed foot for her to trip on at the head of the stairs. Maybe even the truth might do it: She could tell Charlotte about more than her boyfriend—she could add the girls.

"Are you really going to get your ear pierced today?" Charlotte asked one day.

Evelyn had forgotten. "Sure," she answered. "Why not?" She already had a hole in each lobe, but she was thinking of adding another at the top of her left ear. She wanted a silver ring like the one she'd seen on a young woman with very short curly blond hair who wore black jeans and a black leather jacket—a woman Evelyn wanted to know, or be.

Charlotte flipped her long hair off her shoulders. "I could never do that," she said. "What'll Hal think when he sees it?"

"It's none of his business," Evelyn answered as Charlotte followed her across the street.

"But he's your fiancé!" said Charlotte. They went into the alley behind an old drugstore, which was now a record shop called Fountain Music.

"Boyfriend," Evelyn corrected, even though she'd told Charlotte they were engaged last week, when she'd moved into his apartment.

Upstairs from the record store, with an entrance in the alley, was the piercing parlor. On the door was a heart-shaped plaque with a picture of an earlobe pierced by an arrow. "Pierce My Heart—Sweet 206" was written across the top. Evelyn felt laughter, hysterical and unstoppable, rising from her toes. She clutched Charlotte's arm and sputtered, "Do you think they mean suite? Suite, my sweet?"

"What?" asked Charlotte, opening the door. They started up the long wooden staircase.

"The way they spelled it. Suite two-oh-six, s-w-e-e-t. On a heart." Having to explain made her stop laughing. They walked down a long hallway lined with unmarked doors which, years ago, had opened into doctors' offices.

Charlotte sniffed. "This is like where some *abortionist* would have an office," she said.

On a door at the end of the hall there was a sign identical

to the heart-shaped one on the alley door. Evelyn grabbed Charlotte's hand and pushed the door open.

Inside, everything gleamed white and chrome. A receptionist wearing a low-cut white blouse sat behind a desk putting address cards into a Rolodex. Her dark hair was pulled back into a bun, and her fingers were tipped with dark red nails. When she looked up, Evelyn felt as if she could fall into her bottomless dark eyes. The woman stared calmly back at her. A red glow filled the room as the sun dipped behind the brick building opposite the window.

"She wants her ear pierced," said Charlotte, breaking their silent communion.

Evelyn now smiled at the receptionist whose own earlobes were smooth and unadorned. "An additional hole. Here." She indicated the desired point at the side of her left ear, near the top. "I want to stick a ring right there."

The receptionist nodded. "Did you bring your own?" she asked. Something flickered when she opened her mouth, a flash of light the origin of which Evelyn couldn't quite identify.

"I've been thinking of doing it," she explained. "I just haven't found the right ring yet."

The receptionist pulled open a desk drawer and took out several velvet-covered boards on which earrings of gold and silver were displayed. "You've definitely come to the right place," she said.

There were rings, round studs, and studs shaped like hearts, moons, stars, fish, shells and peace symbols, a few glittering with jewels. The woman pointed to a silver ring engraved with a design of entwined black lines, and said, "This one's good." Light flashed off her tongue again, but now she left her mouth open so Evelyn could see there was something on her tongue that glittered in the light from the lamp she tilted to shine on the jewelry. Evelyn stared harder, drawn into that pink mouth.

The receptionist stuck out her tongue. "Do you like it?"

Evelyn drew closer, and saw the tiny gold frog perched there, with eyes made of two ruby chips. She felt herself start to breathe again. "Nice," she said, almost hypnotized by the woman's eyes, which now seemed to have a flash of red in them, like a bad photograph.

"This is a claddagh design," the woman continued, balancing the silver ring on her fingertip. "It's Irish."

Evelyn nodded. "Okay."

"Twenty-five bucks," said the receptionist as she dropped it into a miniature plastic bag and sealed the top before handing it to Evelyn. "Give this to the doctor. And it's another thirty dollars for the piercing."

Evelyn made out the check. The receptionist looked at it closely, as though memorizing it, before she put it into the desk drawer. Charlotte, watching, had said nothing.

She felt her heart thump as the woman led her into a small office and invited her to have a seat. "Will you still be here when I come out?" Evelyn asked, hoping to get a glimpse of that golden frog again.

"Maybe," said the receptionist, flashing her tongue as she left the room.

A man in a white lab coat with the sleeves rolled up above his elbows came in before Evelyn had a chance to sit down. His hair was dyed an unnatural shade of bright yellow.

"Hi, I'm David. Where can we stick you today?"

Evelyn was still thinking about the tiny frog's ruby eyes, and didn't reply for a minute.

"You can sit up or lie down on the examining table, your choice," he said with a smile. Evelyn doubted he was any kind of doctor, no matter what his receptionist claimed. She decided to lie down. In this position she couldn't see him, but could hear the rattle of instruments and water running.

"Now," he said. "What do you want done?"

She pointed to the spot near the top of her left ear.

"There," she said. "I want this ring there." She uncurled her fist to hand him the plastic bag with the earring in it. After he took it, she heard something splash into liquid.

"I'm not at all sure that you'd want a ring in that spot," the man said. "It might stick straight out from your head, you know. Lower down it would work better. Or for that spot, we can exchange this for a stud."

"I want the hoop, right there. I want it to stick out."

He didn't respond. Something cold and wet touched the side of her ear. "Liquid Novocain," he said, "just like the dentist uses to numb your gums before he gives you the shot."

She felt him pull her numbed ear to one side, push it, then push it again.

"There," he said, fumbling with her ear some more. "Done."

She reached for her ear, feeling the ring in its side, not quite as close to the top as she would have liked.

She sat up slowly and swung her legs over the side of the table. He held up a mirror so she could see the claddagh earring, sticking out only slightly.

"It looks good. I like the way it hangs." He sounded surprised.

"I really wanted it higher, so it would stick out more." She lifted the ring with one finger.

"Careful," he said. "You can't feel it yet, but that's an open sore. The Novocain will be gone in a few minutes, and it might hurt a bit for a day or two. Some people feel pain more than others." He opened a drawer and gave her a sample bottle of Binaca mouthwash. "This is antiseptic," he told her. "Put four drops on the piercing three times a day. If it gets infected anyway, see your doctor."

"Were you ever a dentist?" she asked.

He stared at her.

She grinned as she slid off the table. "Just asking."

He turned his back on her to wash his hands. Her ear was already beginning to tingle. When she walked back to the waiting room, the receptionist's chair was empty. Charlotte sat alone, flipping the pages of a magazine.

"Where's . . . ?" Evelyn gestured toward the empty chair behind the desk.

"Gone, I guess. It's after five. What do you care?"

Evelyn's tongue felt fuzzy and her ear ached. With Charlotte behind her, she walked down the narrow stairs and out the door, her ear throbbing with each step.

"Did it hurt?" asked Charlotte.

"Not a bit when he did it," Evelyn said. Her jaw felt tight. She wondered why he hadn't given her a real shot of Novocain so she could get home before the pain hit. This was worse than when her sister had pierced her lobes with nothing but a cork and a needle.

On the street the sun seemed overly bright, even as low as it was. Behind her, Charlotte, back to her usual self, chattered like a bird at sunrise. Two men getting out of a car stared at them as they marched by.

Both Evelyn's ears ached now, the right in sympathy with the left. To distract herself, she nudged Charlotte. "Hey, what do you bet when that guy stands up he'll have his dick out?" she whispered.

"No!" But Charlotte giggled as she looked back at the men. "Evelyn, why do you say things like that?"

There was a cafe on the corner with windows open to the street. "I need a drink," said Evelyn.

"I need dinner." Charlotte's eyes raked the room once they were inside. Evelyn sat down at a table, and Charlotte followed.

"I'll buy. What'll you have?" Evelyn's ear pulsed in time with the music from the jukebox in the corner.

Charlotte smiled at one of the guys at the next table while Evelyn went to the counter and ordered two gin and tonics and, for Charlotte, a slice of quiche.

"I don't want this, why'd you get it?" asked Charlotte as Evelyn put the plate in front of her with the drink, which

Charlotte picked up and took with her as she moved over to the next table.

Evelyn took a long swallow of the gin, which did nothing for her ear.

"Hi." The breathy syllable seemed to come from someplace inside her head. A woman sat down in Charlotte's vacated chair, shaking her long black hair while unzipping a black leather jacket.

Evelyn focused her eyes on the line between the woman's breasts. "Hey," she said.

"I'm from Pierce My Heart, remember? I just sold you that ring." She pointed at Evelyn's ear.

"Oh," said Evelyn, feeling her mouth stretch into a smile. The throbbing in her ear receded as she waited for the receptionist, who sat stirring a glass of rum and Coke, to open her mouth and make the golden frog dance.

"I'm Rebecca," she said. "I remember you're Evelyn. From the check you wrote."

Evelyn saw flashes of gold, of jewels, of white teeth as brilliant as the frog.

"Listen," Rebecca continued. "I'm thinking you must be in pain, right?"

Evelyn took another gulp of gin. "Not so bad now that you're here." she answered. "The occasional twinge."

"Well, I brought you this. I knew you'd come in here—people usually do after a piercing. I'll bet he just told you to take aspirin, but I've got something better." Rebecca took a tiny plastic bag out of her purse, and waved it under Evelyn's nose. There were two white pills inside.

"I'll give you these, and I can get you more if you want. They're a low dose of morphine; nothing's better."

Evelyn's pain was already receding at the sight of those pills. When Rebecca pushed the little bag closer, Evelyn took the bag, opened it, and balanced one of the pills on her tongue, washing it down with another mouthful of gin. "You're sure this is okay? With the gin and all?"

"Oh, it'll be fine," said Rebecca, taking a sip of her drink. "It'd take a lot more than that to addict you, if that's what you're worried about. Take the other one, too."

Evelyn heard her golden frog click against the glass. She swallowed the second pill, then reached into her pocket. "You know what he gave me? Mouthwash!" They both laughed as she shook the little bottle of Binaca in Rebecca's face. "Think I should drink it?"

"No, no. It's a great topical, for cuts and infections. Put some on your ear every day, even if it's not infected, just to be sure it'll stay clean."

The music was starting to overpower the throbbing of her ear, which Evelyn took as a sign that the pills were working. When she picked up her drink again, her fingertips felt numb. She looked over at Charlotte, who frowned at her before turning back to the man she was talking to. After a minute, they got up and moved to a space near the middle of the room where people were beginning to dance.

"Do you dance?" Rebecca let her tongue dangle into her glass as she looked into Evelyn's eyes.

"Sure." Evelyn took Rebecca's hand and led her to where the dancers were. There were all sorts of couples—Charlotte and her man, women with women, men with men and with women. A mixed bar.

Evelyn, accustomed to straight bars or men's or women's bars, was amused. Charlotte glared at her as she and Rebecca danced together, Rebecca moving her arms and legs in a series of articulated jerks to the music, Evelyn swaying in place, feeling a pleasant level of dizziness as she kept her eyes on Rebecca's snug black jeans. Hal liked women in tight jeans, too, and black was his favorite color. This woman had promise.

Rebecca licked her lips while she danced, giving Evelyn tantalizing flashes of the elusive frog. She wondered what it would feel like to take a tongue pierced with hard gold inside her own mouth, or what the frog's ruby eyes might do to her clit and cunt. The thought of pain was strangely exciting.

Oh, where am I going now? Evelyn wondered, imagining herself dancing with Hal and Rebecca together, the hoop bouncing at the top of her ear. Charlotte maneuvered closer to her on the dance floor, close enough to hiss in her ear, "What *is* this place? Do you always come here?" before moving away with her partner, not waiting for an answer.

"You like my frog, don't you?" Rebecca teased when they were back at the table. She stuck out her tongue, then quickly pulled it in. "I like having this because guys don't look at my breasts, you know? They fixate on my mouth." She raised her arms so Evelyn could see the bounce of her breasts, could see that they were free beneath the white silk of her blouse.

When the music stopped, Evelyn's ear still throbbed, much as if it had its own heart. Now the pain seemed to belong to someone else. Rebecca ordered another rum and Coke, then shook her head at Evelyn and said, "With what I gave you, you really shouldn't have another."

Rebecca pointed at the quiche. "Are you going to eat this?"

"No," said Evelyn. "You have it." She watched Rebecca's breasts rub against the silk blouse as she picked up the plate. She ate it in small, quick bites, her fork occasionally clinking against the frog. "Don't you worry you might scratch the gold? Or the eyes might fall out?" Evelyn asked.

"They won't. And if they did, it wouldn't hurt to swallow them." Rebecca took a swig of the rum and Coke. "I just have to be careful to rinse after I eat. Alcohol's good." She took another swallow, swishing it around in her mouth first. "Coke's great, or beer—the foaming action, you know? And Binaca every day. And once a week I take it out and soak it in alcohol."

Evelyn wasn't listening; instead, she was trying to get her drugged and fuzzy mind to decide what to do. Should she take Rebecca home with her? Would Hal really like the threesome they'd talked about a couple of times? Or should she spend time alone with Rebecca first? She couldn't seem to remember how to seduce someone. What were her lines?

"So," Rebecca was saying, "who goes home with whom?"

Evelyn's mind snapped to order. Having Rebecca take charge of this seduction hadn't been the plan. "How about your place?" she said.

Rebecca grinned.

"But first I need to make a call."

Evelyn walked across the floor bouncing to the music on the soles of her feet, feeling like she was flying. She pointed to the phone by the bathroom when anyone tried to dance with her, and kept moving. Suddenly Charlotte's faced loomed over her. "All right, are you gay?" she asked. "Why didn't you tell me? Is Hal really a woman? Is everything you say a lie?"

Evelyn felt her own mouth drop open. "You just never ask the right questions," she said. "And now I'm looking for a phone. See you later." *Good response*, she thought, praising herself as she bopped away from Charlotte towards the phone. With any luck, Charlotte would spread the rumor, plus never speak to her again. All the guys in their class were gay; even the instructor probably was. She'd be in while Charlotte and her gossip would be out.

When she dialed, she got Hal's new answering machine with both their voices on it, chanting the greeting in a duet that embarrassed her as she listened. Hal must be working late. Her mind now rushed past the drug haze as she decided what to reveal in the message and what to conceal. She told him she was out drinking with friends from class and would be home late. She told him she might have a surprise for him, then hung up. She worried she'd been too abrupt. She should have told him she loved him, she should have told him how late she might be, and whom she might be bringing home. She wasn't used to living with a lover.

She made up her mind to leave Rebecca at midnight and save the threesome for another time.

She made her way back to the table, sticking close to the walls this time, avoiding Charlotte while keeping her eyes on Rebecca. When Evelyn crept up behind her and put her hands on her shoulders, Rebecca jumped.

"It's just me," said Evelyn as she sat down, feeling more awake than she had when she'd left the table. "And I'm yours until midnight."

Rebecca fiddled with her empty glass, turning it upside down onto the story plate to watch the last drops of her drink soak the quiche crumbs.

"You see, I just moved in with my boyfriend," Evelyn explained. "We're open, we both have other lovers, but I have to plan now."

Rebecca twirled the glass, which clinked against the plate. "Okay. My place is fine. What about your girlfriend?"

Evelyn laughed at the idea of Charlotte as a girlfriend— even a straight, chaste one. "Charlotte? She's just someone from the cooking school I go to. I wouldn't call her a friend." When Evelyn stood up and put on her coat, Rebecca followed. They walked single file out the door, Evelyn in the lead.

"Where are we going?" she asked when they were outside.

"Not far," Rebecca answered. "Two blocks up the hill, turn right."

Evelyn led the way, and after they turned, Rebecca directed her to a three-story brick apartment building. They climbed the stairs to the third floor because Rebecca said the elevator was out of order so often that it wasn't even worth trying. When they reached Rebecca's door, she stepped in front of Evelyn with her key to let them in, and switched on the light.

A long room came into view, with a large bay window at the far end, and, near the door, a small stove, sink, and refrigerator that reminded Evelyn of the kitchen play area in kindergarten. There was a cupboard over the sink and a small table against the wall flanked by two chairs. Against the opposite wall was a bed that was not unlike the top half of a bunk bed with a ladder leading up to it and, in the space beneath, a desk scattered with books and papers.

They stood in the center of the room. "I like it," Evelyn finally said. "It's a doll's house, with your whole life at your fingertips. Do you go to school?"

"Off and on. Not now, though. Don't laugh, but I'm writing a novel."

"What about?"

"I can't decide. I'm just gathering material about piercing. Sex. Life."

Evelyn wondered about finding herself turned into material, and, if so, how best to present herself. She watched

Rebecca fill a tea kettle with water and balance it on the mini-stove, turning on a small gas burner. Evelyn sat down at the table, artfully arranging her coat on the chair behind her, leaning her elbows on the table, resting her chin winningly on her folded hands. "Shall we go upstairs?" she asked in a low voice, waving her hand in the direction of the loft bed.

Rebecca still had her coat on. She took two cups from the cupboard above the sink, set them on the table, and put a tea bag in each. "Herbal, no caffeine," she said firmly, not offering a choice. Then she took off her coat and draped it over the other kitchen chair before sitting.

Evelyn yawned. "I'm drugged, I need caffeine."

"Let's see that ear." Rebecca brushed Evelyn's hair out of the way. "Give me the mouthwash."

Evelyn handed her the vial, which she upended, sprinkling a cold, stinging drop onto the sore ear. The pain was far away, as though in another body Evelyn had inhabited in some former life. "Thank you, Nurse Rebecca," she murmured, reaching out to take one of Rebecca's hands, which were busily arranging the Binaca on the table, first near the salt and pepper shakers shaped like chickens, then sliding it closer to Evelyn, who picked it up and put it back in her pocket.

"I should tell you I'm new at this," Rebecca said, placing the chickens so their beaks faced each other as if they were about to fight, or kiss.

"New at what?" Evelyn asked, thinking, *Oh no, oh no.*

"At women. Sex with them. Us," said Rebecca. "But I felt

you seemed. . . ." She spread her arms, then dropped them in her lap.

Inexperience made Evelyn nervous. *You picked me up in a bar, and now you want me to seduce you?* she felt like shouting, but didn't. This was when she could have told Rebecca she'd never made love to a woman either. The fact of Hal, her boyfriend-fiancé, would help make this lie believable. Or, closer to the truth, she might explain she was really looking for a woman they could share, just for the experience. Or, she could have just finished her tea and left.

But she didn't.

"My first time with a girl was in high school," she confessed. "We danced together at a party. All the girls did, because there weren't enough boys. We were just fourteen, and one dance led to another, you know? We practiced kissing so we'd know what to do when we started dating guys, but after a while I started to wonder what exactly we needed them for."

Rebecca smiled.

"It was fun," Evelyn went on. "No big deal." She was not, of course, being entirely truthful. "With guys, it always gets complicated, you know?" She looked at her watch and saw that it was already nine o'clock.

"Like, I have this primary partner now, Hal." She liked the words "primary partner," which explained so much while revealing so little. She reached to the radio on a shelf above the table and switched it on, guessing Rebecca would have it set to something they could dance to. But what she heard surprised her: it was a vintage oldies station, with a man, accompanied by a big band, singing, "All of me, why don't you take all of me. . . . "

Rebecca jumped up from the table. "I took swing lessons," she said. "Here, I'll show you."

The next number was faster. Evelyn found herself swinging and twirling at the ends of Rebecca's arms, dancing around and away from her, almost hitting the walls of the apartment, then being pulled back again, carried away by song after song until she began to wish for something less jazzy, some old crooner, slow and moody. When one finally came on, she rocked back and forth in Rebecca's arms, then found her arms around Rebecca, until they were kissing, swaying, with Rebecca's heart pounding against Evelyn's breast.

It had been a while since Evelyn had seen the gold frog, so she parted Rebecca's lips with her tongue, reaching and probing until she felt it. She sucked, moving the frog back and forth across her upper lip, while wondering how to get Rebecca to climb the stairs to her bed. It would be a conscious act, a decision to go to bed with a woman, that Evelyn now wasn't sure Rebecca was ready for. But then Rebecca danced Evelyn into a corner of the room and behind the bed, where pillows were stacked against the wall. Sinking down, she pulled Evelyn with her.

They lay side by side, Rebecca thrusting her tongue into Evelyn's mouth. Evelyn played with the pearl buttons on Rebecca's blouse, slowly loosening them, unbuttoning the blouse, fingers slipping onto breasts. Rebecca's tongue stopped as Evelyn touched her hardening nipples. The tongue withdrew and Evelyn went after it, pushing Rebecca into the pillows, but Rebecca turned her head away.

"What comes next?" she asked, pretending innocence again.

"Don't ask, just do." Evelyn was annoyed. "It's the same as with guys, except the dildo isn't attached. If you want one, that is."

"I don't have one," Rebecca said.

Evelyn began to lick her nipples. "Who needs it? Tongues and fingers work great." Evelyn sucked one breast, then the other.

"This is so like high school," Rebecca sighed. "I mean, I love it when nothing has to happen."

"What do you mean 'nothing'?" Evelyn sat up and unzipped Rebecca's jeans, sliding them off her hips. She didn't wear underpants. Evelyn gave a low whistle. "Hey," she said, "isn't that uncomfortable?" She sniffed the wet seam of Rebecca's jeans.

"You get used to it," said Rebecca. "Sometimes when it rubs just right, it's great. You have to be careful where the seam goes, that's all."

Evelyn's fingers slid lightly across Rebecca's fur, coming to rest at the tip of her clit, then sliding under, sliding in, pressing one finger, there, just inside her cunt at the base of the clit while Rebecca started to breathe faster. Slowly, Evelyn lowered her mouth and sucked, massaging a circular pattern with her finger inside Rebecca, feeling the timeless pleasure of another woman's arousal. Rebecca accepted the movement of her fingers, first one, then two, then three, until her belly began to ripple and Evelyn could feel her cunt suck her fingers, pulling them deeper inside.

"*Ahhh*," moaned Rebecca. And then she seemed to remember the role she was playing as she drew her legs together, propped herself up, and looked quizzically at Evelyn. "And now, what do you want me to do?"

Evelyn stretched out beside her, toying with a breast. "I think you know very well," she challenged, looking deep into Rebecca's eyes.

Rebecca stared back.

Waiting to see what she would do, Evelyn was definitely aroused, swollen, wet, ready for the touch of a hand, hers or Rebecca's, or even Hal's cock, surely waiting at home by now. Maybe Rebecca had a car and would drive her there with one hand inside Evelyn's unzipped jeans. She pictured that scene, getting wetter and more swollen by the minute as she imaged her lover driving her to her boyfriend, and then the three of them sloshing around on Hal's king-size waterbed.

Rebecca reached down to unzip Evelyn's jeans, skillfully pulling them off her hips, then lowered her face to Evelyn's underpants, peach silk, which she'd put on that morning without knowing why she wanted to wear them. Rebecca pulled down the silk panties and touched the golden frog to Evelyn's swollen clit, which sent a jolt of anticipatory electricity across her belly. She tensed, worried about being hurt by that frog, but Rebecca was careful, the tip of her tongue controlled, smooth, tentative, as she gently rolled the frog along the side of Evelyn's clit.

Rebecca lifted her head. "Okay?" she asked, breathlessly, like Marilyn Monroe in some old movie.

"Oh, yeah," breathed Evelyn.

It was more than she'd expected, Rebecca's tongue carefully working its way around her clit, up and down the shaft, across the tip, while Evelyn held the image of the frog in her mind, willing Rebecca to be careful as she nudged it against the side of her clit until she felt a quiver inside that grew until her skin tingled.

"Don't stop, don't stop!" she cried as she always did when she came, meaning that she didn't want the feeling to stop, but Rebecca took that as an order and kept on until Evelyn finally had to push her away.

They lay side by side, Rebecca's hand feeling Evelyn's breasts through her sweater. They kissed, tasting themselves on each other's lips. Rebecca licked Evelyn's ear, rolling her tongue carefully around the ring. "Saliva is antiseptic, too," she whispered, blowing Evelyn's ear dry. "And I forgot to use the Binaca. I'll show you sometime what it's really good for."

Evelyn suddenly felt like running. "It's almost midnight. I've got to get going! Do you have a car?"

"No." Rebecca sat up.

Evelyn was relieved. She wasn't sure now that she wanted Hal to meet Rebecca. "That's all right, I can catch the bus."

Jeans on, zippers zipped, coats buttoned. They were ready to go in minutes.

"The bus runs all night," said Rebecca, "but only every hour after midnight. I think we'll just make the next one."

"You don't have to come with me, really," Evelyn protested.

"But I want to," Rebecca answered. "I can't let you wait on the street alone." She took Evelyn's hand and led her out the door, down the steps, and through the lobby with its cheap mirrors out to the street. They retraced their route down the hill past the bar, which shook with loud music, to the bus stop in front of Fountain Music. Soft jazz spilled into the street to inspire midnight, midweek shopping. There was a stained-glass window above the entrance with "RX" encircled by a snake, and "Drugs and Sodas" written beneath.

The recipe for a perfect life, Evelyn thought. Through the front window, she could see Charlotte with the man from the bar, going through a bin of sale albums. She looked up briefly, then looked back down as soon as she recognized Evelyn.

Rebecca wouldn't let go of her hand, which made Evelyn impatient for the bus to come so that Rebecca would leave, go back home, and climb the ladder to her loft, to the bed where Evelyn had not been invited, though she had imagined them climbing up there together. She looked down the street until she saw the yellow eyes of the bus turn the corner by the bar.

"Here it comes!" she cried, glad they weren't going to have to wait an hour.

"Don't go," Rebecca whispered in her ear. "You could stay with me. When will I see you again?"

"Soon," said Evelyn.

"You know where to find me." She stuck her golden frog deep into Evelyn's mouth.

The bus stopped, and Evelyn pulled herself away to jump on. Rebecca waved, running up the street until the bus roared past her.

When Evelyn looked back, she thought the streetlight caught a flash of the frog's ruby eyes in Rebecca's open, panting mouth. The glow seemed to pierce her heart as the bus came to a halt for a moment, then moved on.

A GUIDE TO ALIEN DATING

by Leigh Ward

As Jane approached the little group of late-night drinkers huddled around the hotel bar, she cleared her throat softly. It was enough to cause the three men nursing their beers to look up, and since they were already ignoring the shrill demands of the several TV's suspended above their heads, that was no small accomplishment.

She waited a moment, then smiled. They grinned back at her. "Hey," she said.

"Hey," said one of them, the one with the blue teeth and shaved, cross-hatched skull. This was Jeebil.

"What're you going to have?" Redfuss asked her. His ears flapped slowly as he drummed the furry fingers of his third hand on the slick surface of the bar.

"A draft, I guess. But one with a little flavor."

"Try what I've got," Nargo offered. "It's a special for the weekend—a Piltonoid Porter. Nice and malty, you'll like it."

"Okay," she said. "But what's it when it's at home?"

Nargo was offended, as she knew he would be. She could tell because he beetled his aluminum eyebrows before shrugging and turning to signal the bartender.

The trouble with these Armandalian conventions, Jane had long ago decided, was that there was a decided deficiency of humor when it came to even the teeniest intrusion of reality. Sure, it was a Holiday Inn at the intersection of two extremely boring central Pennsylvania highways, but, for such hardcore fans as Nargo, Jeebil and Redfuss, the very idea of Pennsylvania wasn't even open to discussion. If the three of them were there, ipso facto, they were inhabiting the Thirty-seventh Realm of Armandal in the Ascendancy of Lord Grentvin, and, as Fifth-Degree Saber Savants, they were a trio to be reckoned with. End of story.

Normally, Jane, who worked as an editor at the publishing house that kept in print all the books of the never-ending and always profitable Armandal Chronicles (there were sixty-seven to date, with a sixty-eighth having been launched with a party that very evening), played along. It was her job, for one thing, and who was she to argue with the fantasies of a vast number of geeks around the world—the Japanese, of course, were the worst, that is, the most tirelessly enthusiastic—who helped pay her salary? The fact that the Armandalian world—or at least its card-holding, convention-going contingent—was entirely male didn't matter, of course, since, after all these years of watching them do things like strapping on weird prostheses and staining their teeth, how could she take any of them seriously?

She knew that Jeebil was an investment banker in San Francisco, Redfuss a senator's legislative assistant, and that Nargo taught philosophy at Rutgers; she also knew that they were, respectively, divorced, separated and single. (Redfuss's marriage had been breaking up at the time of the previous year's convention in Illinois; she'd let him cry on her shoulder, but that was all she'd let him do.) On paper, each of them was a catch—somehow the Thirty-seventh Realm of Armandal snared promising youth at an early age, bright boys destined to succeed in life—but Jane wasn't buying any of it.

Herself still living alone at nearly forty, and a veteran of the kind of short-term, long-to-actually-end affairs that passed for relationships nowadays, she'd need to knock back more than a few Piltonoid Porters before she could imagine kissing a Saber Savant, let alone fucking one.

"Here's your drink, Jane," said Redfuss. She could see Nargo was still sulking a little. She raised her glass. "Cheers, you guys, it's always good to see you." And even if she didn't mean it, she knew she meant it in a way they might not understand. Continuity, tradition, ritual: they were all different ways of saying habit, and, retarded adolescents though they might be, they were her retarded adolescents after so many years.

The Piltonoid Porter went down smoothly. Nargo had been right, it was pretty tasty, even if the conceit that it wasn't just a Beck's Dark was one she had no desire to maintain. It was late, after all, and it had been a long day.

The problem with Armandal, she thought, not for the first time, was that it was a kitchen sink of an ongoing saga. From rocketeers to knights on chargers, from little green men to monstrous clanking robots, from tentacled medusas to busty biker babes, there was something for everyone. That was its glory (if you were marketing the series) and its shame (if you had any literary aspirations). And while Jane understood its popularity, not actually objecting to it on grounds of taste, what she did mind—she couldn't help it—was that it was a pulp slumgullion of entirely accidental creation.

Van Loon Brown, who'd written the first fifteen Armandal titles, had died suddenly while in the midst of roughing out number sixteen. It had been a tragedy not just for his nearest and dearest, but for all his foreign license-holders, not to mention Pursell & Peters who for the past seventeen years had been Jane's employer and controlled the estate. Since then, Van Loon Brown had been turned into a Pursell & Peters house name, with almost anyone who could put 105,000 words to paper producing an Armandal novel, including, at one point—or so Jane had heard but could never quite confirm—an ambitious maintenance man.

Continuity, in this way, had gone out the window.

So why, she silently sent up the rhetorical question, did these otherwise extremely smart guys—that is, Nargo, Redfuss, Jeebil and their fellow cosmetically challenged convention-goers—base such a large part of their lives on the content of nearly seventy goofy books?

"I give up," she inadvertently answered herself aloud.

Sighing, she rolled her eyes. She then blushed, despite the fact that no one had even noticed her. Whatever her private opinion might be, she prided herself on her ability to maintain a professional mien. Besides, she had spent the better part of two decades in and around the precincts of Armandal and, like it or not, probably had to be considered an honorary citizen.

"Jane," said Jeebil, looking at her with blue-toothed concern, "are you okay?"

"Yep, I am. Just fine." She took another swallow of beer, closing her eyes as she did so. A second later, when she opened them, there was someone standing before her whom she'd never seen before. He was—she blinked again, then looked at him a second time—quite remarkable.

She examined him as politely and quickly as she could. However, her first impression seemed to hold: what was remarkable about him was the fact—like the dog that didn't bark in the night—that there was nothing whatsoever remarkable about him at all. Unless you counted the way he was raising one (normal) eyebrow almost to his hairline as he stared back at her with obvious amusement.

"Wow," she said. "You could qualify for the Eyebrow Olympics, I'll bet." It was all she could think of. Pretty lame.

But he smiled, and, as it turned out, his smile was pretty remarkable, too. Jane's insides did a pleasurable flip-flop that seemed entirely independent of the Piltonoid Porter she'd just finished.

"Thanks," he said. "At least I think that's intended as a

compliment. If not, I'll go ahead and take it as one. But I'm not actually sure I could last when it comes to the training part. I know it's only eyebrows . . . the problem is, I'm . . . kind of lazy."

"Don't listen to him," said Nargo, waggling a glued-on aluminum eyebrows for emphasis. "He's actually one of the hardest-working doctors I know."

"Medical doctor?" she couldn't help asking.

"Not exactly. I was. That is, I am. But these days I just do policy. Consulting. Getting a chance to put my two cents in on the big health care issues. You know, try to make a difference." He had straight dark hair that flopped into his eyes, and front teeth that were just slightly crooked, adding to the boyish charm of his smile.

"Wouldn't you be making a difference each and every time you examined a patient?" It seemed a fair question to her.

"You're right," he said. "But that's only one kind of difference. Right now I'm interested in a different kind of difference, you might say."

"Okay," she said. "By the way, I'm Jane."

"I know. I'm Dan."

"How come you're not Peetwee or Samjam? Or Thain Colt? Or some other Armandal character? Like our pals here."

"Because I've never read any of the books, that's why. I just came over to the hotel to have a drink with Phil—we went to school together. I'm attending a conference at the college down the road, and we were e-mailing last week and somehow discovered both of us were going to be here this weekend." Phil was Nargo, of course.

"Oh," she said, unable to come up with a wittier reply.

"Are you ready for another beer?" he asked. She looked down at her glass. "Sure, but I might not be able to finish it. I'm getting a little sleepy."

"You're an editor, right?"

"Um-hm. Mostly contemporary fiction, and sometimes I work on the latest Armandal manuscript, depending on who's written it."

He paid the bartender for the drinks just set down in front of them. "Thanks," Jane said. She reached for the bowl of pretzel sticks. "Dinner was a while ago," she explained. "But, on the other hand, I'm always hungry."

Nargo, who'd been listening, now broke in, "It's good to see a woman who drinks something beside Diet Coke. Jane kind of reminds me of Elfana the Leaf Queen." But when Dan didn't exhibit much reaction to this Armandalian comparison, his old friend quickly enlarged upon the analogy. "You know . . ." He glanced at Jane a little apprehensively, then, said, "Sexy, but in a sort of soulful way."

She laughed. "At least you didn't say I was like Twilma Overgone." Dan still looked blank. "Three eyes, four breasts and a mustache," Jeebil enlightened him.

Redfuss nodded his agreement. "Jane doesn't even have to shave."

"Okay, okay," she told them in mock indignation. "I think we've discussed my charms long enough."

Dan, to her surprise, motioned her toward him conspiratorially. She leaned forward, and he whispered in her ear, so softly she almost didn't hear: "I disagree."

∽∾

What were the possible scenarios? If men are from Mars and women from Venus—and the occasional oddballs are from Armandal—how does this story end? Even as it was happening to her, Jane was posing to herself the questions that any wary female must take into account. It was true that motels—even Holiday Inns—generate a certain amount of free-floating sexual heat in their very prepackaged anonymity. But let's say she never saw Dan again—there was still the Armandal gossip grapevine to contend with. They'd know, somehow.

And, heaven knows, there was also the old "would he respect her in the morning?" business to deal with as well. The solution, she suddenly decided, despite feeling incredibly turned-on by the adorable Dan's whispering in her ear, was to play it safe. She's just have to miss out on his bedside manner. Would she respect *herself* come daylight? That was always the *real* worry.

"I think it's time for me to turn in," she told them. "It was great to meet you," she said to Dan. "Here's my card."

He seemed disappointed. But what did he expect?

"Thanks." He looked at it, and even turned it over, examining the back. Did he think she might have written her room number on it?

"See you guys at breakfast!" she said to her stalwart trio of Sabre Savants. The convention would be breaking up in the morning. In other corners of the room, as she walked out, she saw various familiar Armandal characters, all absorbed in their own discussions and oblivious to the stares of the ordinary barflies. They were undoubtedly high-powered attorneys and stockbrokers, bank presidents and high school principals back home, but here they were creatures of a crazed, cloistered universe.

"Good night!" she paused to say to one intense group who, over a pitcher of margaritas, were having a spirited argument. "G'night, Jane!" called out one of them, a fellow with a set of glow-in-the-dark fangs protruding from the center of his forehead.

She waved, took one more look around the bar, and headed for the elevator.

❦

She brushed her teeth. Splashed water on her face. Rubbed in moisturizer. Made a stab at cleaning her nails. Took a couple of aspirin. Peed. Thought about calling her apartment and checking her messages, but didn't have the energy. Too tired even to read, she switched off the light and lay still, listening to the faint institutional hum that permeated the air. Somewhere a toilet flushed, then another. Deep inside the walls a shower was running. She pulled a pillow against her stomach, clutching it, felt the sheets twisting up around her legs. The small world beneath the covers that was her body seemed to transmit and attract a heightened reality. She could even hear the red digital numbers of the clock radio changing, or so she thought. Her nose itched. A corner of the pillow gave off a not-unpleasant, slightly sour scent. Shit, did she have to pee again? A car's tires squealed outside the window. Another toilet flushed. Her heartbeat came up out of the darkness. Her breathing shifted. The darkness turned faint, like smoke, but her eyes were closed.

Jane was asleep.

⸎

Blue. A blue man was lifting the sheet and reaching for her. She rolled away instinctively, but he took hold of her leg and slid his hand up inside her thigh. His touch was gentle. He stroked first the tender skin of one leg, then the other, running the edge of his azure finger lightly up and down, up and down, up and down. From her toes to her hips, he covered her flesh with the lightest of caresses. Lingering over her crevices, almost brushing against her dripping vaginal lips, leaning down to blow soft air on her belly, he seemed tireless. She moaned and stretched, pushing against him, feeling as if she might be blue herself now, wherever he had touched her.

Suddenly a second figure was beside her. She couldn't be certain, but he seemed to be casting a silver iridescence over everything near him. As the blue man continued to encourage sensation along the borders of her cunt, the silver one positioned himself to suck lovingly on her breasts. He smelled wonderful, like the first breath of a frosty morning, yet she wasn't cold. Every few minutes—or was it hours?—he would stop and pinch her nipples, then roll them between his fingers.

Then, without any warning, except for an expelled breath that she barely heard, there was another presence. Holding her head, he delicately massaged her temples. His fingers were covered in a soft fur, which she could feel on her cheeks. Now, one of them—she wasn't sure who—took her hand and clasped it around his cock. Her breasts, freed of any touch, ached exquisitely.

Why was the room so dark that she could see none of them clearly? She sighed as she felt his hardness throb in her grasp, then pull away. He rubbed himself slowly against her face and lips, and, with her body straining toward the farthest edges of the excitement she was lost in, she welcomed him into her mouth.

At that very moment, she felt herself being penetrated elsewhere: first with one finger, then two, stroking and rubbing, and finally, there was the fullness of a warm, smooth cock sliding into her cunt. Oh! she thought as, quickly—too quickly—it was withdrawn. She was still suckling luxuriantly on the one in her mouth. Come back. Did she hear a chuckle? Yet she could feel its tip down there still, like an echo of her need, hesitating at the opening, teasing her, holding her at bay.

When it plunged in again, it was all she could do to breathe, and then, suddenly, her mouth was empty. She moaned again, quivering. Now, whoever had been fucking her—or was it someone new?—began expertly controlling his entry into her, each time pushing farther and farther toward her center. Now, her nipples were still being alternately sucked and pinched, and the tremors and tightness that ran through her were fighting for release. Now, someone was gently rubbing her clitoris, letting the pressure alternate with the careful thrusts.

Slower, for a while. Faster, faster . . . hold on, she thought.

Hold on.

Hold. On.

Oh, my God.

Ohhhh.

⸙

Jane opened her eyes. She could see the outlines of all the furniture and just the merest sliver of daylight at the edge of the heavy fabric that covered the windows. Throwing off the bedclothes, she stood up and stretched, then walked over to pull open the curtains and check out the weather. She felt wonderful, and incredibly relaxed. Laughing at the idea, she wondered if maybe that Piltonoid Porter had done the trick.

Yet, at the same time, she felt anticipatory. What was about to happen? What *had* happened? Emerging from the bathroom, she hesitated as she opened the closet door. The strangest glimmerings of a dream shot through her consciousness, but when she tried to pin it down, to move it from the realm of the blurry to the concrete, it wouldn't come clear. As she zipped up her jeans, the phone rang.

"Hello?"

"Hi, good morning, it's Dan," the voice said. "I know it's early, but I thought I might get you to have lunch with me later on, before you headed back to the city. I'm not heading out of town until this afternoon."

"Hmm," she said. "I don't see why not. They won't miss me."

"Great. Meet me in the lobby at noon. We can go to the coffee shop."

"Okay. See you then."

As she hung up, she smiled to herself. Cool. That's cool. It'll be interesting to see what he's like, if he's as much fun to talk to as he is to look at.

But, at the same time, some little buzzer was pinging in her head.

They won't miss me.

True enough, but it did give her pause, because, all at once, she remembered her dream.

It hadn't been about Dan.

LIFE CLASS

᠊ᢡᢀᠣ᠊

by Georgi Mayr

It was the start of the fall semester and the honors students at The Angelo School had all clustered around the notice board. It was announced there that Douka, the celebrated painter, would preside over the weekly life class that year. Douka. Here. Some of them thought it was a practical joke, and on the first Wednesday they teased Arli, the model, who had already prepared herself, nonchalant and naked, on her small platform in the middle of the room, "What do you feel like, being done by Douka?" Arli gave one of her irritated little shrugs, impatient to be at work. Then the door merely opened and Douka entered.

At first there was silence in the room and then a whisper rippled around. "He looks smaller in the flesh," whispered one girl to a more talented friend. "But the hands, those eyes—" the friend could not stop staring. It was not only for his work that Douka was legendary. His hands were long, broad and strong, and his eyes, deep set and keen, were of an impenetrable color, a muddy blue-green, like a churned-up ocean.

He set up his chair and drawing board quietly and quickly at the back of the room and sat down, seemingly unaware of the impact of his presence. The students took longer than ever to settle, unable to bring out their pencils while he was at their back. Arli, the model, on her dais in the center of the room, shifted her position in slight annoyance as they took so long to get to their work. There was a rasp of displeasure, a click of tongue against teeth from the back of the room, and Douka got up, strode to the dais and adjusted her minutely, turning her ankle a fraction out to precisely where it had been before, and tilting her heart-shaped chin back into the light.

This was the signal to begin. A wave of seriousness swept over the group and at once pencils were raised, heads were down, eyes lifted and lowered, and there was no sound except the soft scratch of pencil on paper. Douka took his shoes off and padded around behind the group looking over their shoulders. He stopped at a student's chair, took the pencil from behind his ear and drew a swift, strong corrective line, the curve of the back of Arli's head. At another's, he crosshatched in shadow to capture the gleam of light from Arli's bright white hair. The student whose page he was attending to sat back and saw his drawing as if for the first time. Later, each asked of the other, "How can I ever do that?" Douka's other skills, manifest in his physical presence, were forgotten as his artistry flowed amongst them.

By the second Wednesday, there were queues for the class and standing room only inside, and by the third there was a waiting list. The students wondered why he was doing this, and someone said that he was preparing for a major show in the autumn, and that this was his discipline, his training.

Once, an older man with a moustache came and stood at the back, silently watching not the students, but Douka as he worked. Douka appeared indifferent, as he was to the queues that waited for him each week. When he arrived, he walked past the line of his fans and into the studio, and got straight to work without a word. Arli, the model, was always there before him and always ready, stripped and waiting. Sometimes, as on that first day, she showed her irritation at the students' slackness, and moved. Then Douka came straight over to her, staring closely, and adjusted her in tiny sure moves as if she were his modeling clay, putting her precisely where she was before.

Over the weeks, Douka's corrective touch came to feel to Arli like a slight, a criticism, an expression of her failure. But her annoyance with the students who were so impressed by him that they could not work forced her to move, to fidget. She tried so hard not to allow the rustling and inattention of her audience move her—she controlled her breathing, held herself in, tried to numb her skin as if it was already securely watched—but she couldn't do it. And if her keen ears picked up the merest whisper about the great man rather than attention to her, to the work, she lapsed and let her flesh go soft.

He'd be in front of her in a second, and would stand there

for a moment and then his wide hands would spread her and lift her and tilt her until she was back where she had first chosen to be.

One day, near the end of the semester, some new students had managed to get in, having bribed their way to the front of the line. They were more rowdy than ever, but somehow their extremeness allowed Arli to achieve complete stillness in spite of them. Douka came over and stood in front of her and examined every inch of her body, the cropped white hair, the bright blue eyes, the little pink mouth, the column of neck, the tilt of creamy shoulder and lift of arm, the light swell of breast and belly, the shadow beneath, and long thigh, arched calf and delicate foot. He adjusted nothing but went to his seat without a word and worked. After some time there arose more of a ripple around the room than usual, and some movement and rustling of chairs.

Douka hadn't got up, hadn't even glanced at the students' work this time. There was a rumble of dismay. But Douka was working. He was pouring his vision of Arli onto the page, and he could not stop. The white hair, the creamy skin, the sheer brightness of feature, there it all was, and now the students, one by one, crept up and looked over his shoulder as he created her on the page. "I don't know how he does it," they exclaimed. "How do you do 'blue' with pencil, and white? I can see how, sometimes, but this glow. I don't know how he can." Neither Douka nor Arli heard anything.

At the end of term, Douka asked Arli to come and model for him in his studio. She accepted. The first time she got ready and sat on the chair where he put her, he took some time to get ready himself and she fidgeted. He stood with his arms folded, staring at her as if he'd never seen her before and then came over: he lifted her limbs with his broad hands, squeezed her creamy thighs open to exactly where he'd put them before, rolled her shoulders back, pushed forward her breasts, laid open her palms and threw back her head. As Douka worked, his head was down, his eyes never lifted from the paper, and he kept at it until there was no light left.

The next time, Arli knew exactly where to place herself, her body, even her skin seeming to have a memory for this, and so she put herself there in perfect readiness. Then, minutely, she drew her chin down, and bowed over her breasts, lowering her arms just a fraction, and closing her creamy thighs. Douka stared. He made a step toward her, then stopped. He knew she'd been ready, and that she'd done this on purpose so that he would mold her.

He stared at her. Her gaze was, as always, indifferent. Then he strode over and fell to his knees in front of her. Those piercing eyes traveled all over her body as the long skillful hands plied her limbs this way and that, opening her and closing her to his eye, and then at last to mouth, and body.

Arli and Douka had lived together for some time when an older man with a moustache, Douka's agent Frank, paid a visit to see how the work was coming for the show. He was starting to collect it together, to find buyers. Douka left him alone to riffle through the sheaves of pictures leaning everywhere against the walls of the studio. He went to lie on the tangled bed behind the easel.

The early pictures of Arli were ravishing. She seemed to glow from the page, to light the eye, to be alive. Frank had already seen these—he had used them as bait for a new set of major buyers in the first place. "Where are the new ones? Where are the rest?"

Douka pulled his hand through his unruly hair and got up from the bed and sat on the edge. Arli was out.

"Is she modeling?"

Douka looked at him as if he were mad. Arli couldn't model now. He could not tolerate other eyes upon her.

"Well," said Frank, "and your eyes? Are they upon her? Is she in the new ones too?" Again, there was that mute gesture from Douka, of his hand through his hair. Frank understood. Douka wasn't working. "And Arli? She's well? And you two—?"

"My friend, my dear old friend, it has never been better. We live in paradise. I have never known anything like it. We *love* all day long."

Frank then said, "You must come and visit. Have a break. Bring her. You must both come. You're a lucky man, my friend."

When Douka had given up the life class, he had insisted that Arli give it up as well. She was needed here in the studio, where all day, every day, she sat for him. She got up, washed, they had breakfast, then she took her clothes off and sat however he arranged her, in whatever pose. Sometimes lying on the tangled sheets of their bed, sometimes with her back to him, leaning over, so that the curve of her spine and the cleft of her buttocks and the little tattoo on one cheek were all he could see.

Sometimes he had her standing for hours with one leg on the hard school chair, so that he could see between her legs, and into her sex. Sometimes he had her cup her breasts at him as if she were offering him food. Sometimes she just stood with her hands drooping by her sides like someone on the side of a road. If she so much as moved her lips, parted them, gasped, he would be on her at once, adjusting, pressing her lips together, rolling out her flesh, parting folds, smoothing crests, patting dry what had become too quickly moist.

And as time went on, the time lessened between her pose for him and her little gasp, or the parting of her lips or the lowering of her eyes or a trembling of her inner leg. And so too did the time disappear between that movement of hers and his bounding over to adjust her, until it happened that almost as soon as he had put her into a pose, almost before he heard her barely stifled gasp, he was over and onto her, spreading and kneading and sucking and lapping at her and they were quite unable to disentangle. Their very skins tingled for the other's touch. But what had been founded in looking expressed itself now in increasingly fervid touch. And the more desire took over, the greater was both their frustration.

After the incredulous passion of the first few weeks and months, they didn't even make love any more, they just posed, and moved, and adjusted. Douka crammed himself hopelessly onto her, moving her, feeling her, unfolding her, folding her away, unable himself to perform on paper or in bed, while she remained simultaneously craving and thwarted.

Frank came a second time on business and noticed the hollow of his friend's eyes as he listened to Douka tell him how happy he was, they both were, how they couldn't leave each other alone, they were so close. And Frank said nothing, but the following day an invitation from him arrived. He confided that he, too, had found a love, someone he'd like Douka to meet. Frank lived on the far side of town, almost in the countryside, so really it would be a trip, their first, and they would stay for a night. Maybe two.

Frank had prepared one of his feasts—a mighty roast, plate after plate of steaming, buttery vegetables, a sumptuous dessert, lashings of wine, fruit, cream and cheeses from some little farm he had discovered on one of his private trips. The new woman, Minna, slight, wiry and hatchet-faced, with tendrils of hair straggling over her face, said and ate very little during the evening. Not Frank's usual type at all, not the usual juicy indulgence. But she laughed when Frank or Douka made a joke and smiled with great wide warmth at Arli. Arli drank too much.

"This is serious?" guessed Douka, when the men went out onto the porch for a smoke.

"Decidedly," Frank said.

"Serious again or serious?"

Frank smiled, "This is it, my friend. We've both found it at once, I do believe."

Douka shifted a little, not knowing why but uncomfortable. When they went back inside Arli and Minna were standing by the window talking, and Douka had to stop himself going straight over and pressing himself over to Arli right there, touching her, pushing her into the position he'd last seen her in. He could not tolerate distance. It was time, anyway, for bed. They were to sleep downstairs in a big square bed, while Frank and Minna were upstairs. They said their goodnights.

In the strange smell of a new bed, Douka was doubly uncomfortable. He tried to cover Arli but she shrugged him off, tired, irritable. It was not her usual irritation at lack of work—she was just annoyed, as if her skin no longer absorbed him but flinched him off, like a horse with a fly. She had drunk too much, she wanted to sleep. Douka lay awake, staring at the marks on the ceiling or leaning on his arm to stare at her and gnawing at his lip. Some time later, he heard their door open and the soft pad of bare feet across the floorboards. Then the woman Minna was at his bedside and sitting beside him. Without a word, she folded back the covers and slid in. Douka leaned on his elbows, raising himself a little in the bed.

"It's lonely up there," she told him. Douka said nothing. Minna just lay there between the two of them, quite stiffly, for the moment. Then she leaned on one arm, straight in front of him, so that they were like two knives.

"She's lovely," she said.

Douka sighed, "Yes," he breathed. Oh yes. The ravishment of his eye.

"A beautifully shaped head," said Minna, looking down at the sleeping form, the white-gold child head on the pillow, the lightly parted rose lips, the thick dark fringe of lash on the pale cheeks.

Douka stirred, raising himself on an elbow, looking down over Minna's shoulder. "See there," he said, "the nape of the neck, and this hollow going into the curve of shoulder." Very gently, he folded back the sheet to show Minna what he meant. "Here, the firmness here that turns into the mound of the breast, see, this one is a little larger, and there is this little mole here—" he traced the shape of the breast, covering the small mole with his forefinger, lightly so as not to touch.

Minna turned slightly, twisting in the bed beside him, and he drew down the sheet a little further from the sleeping girl. Arli was breathing evenly, and a little bubble came through her lightly parted lips as she shifted, her hands flattening on the bed.

"The tiny waist," said Minna, gazing. "And that fine down below the navel, the tight whorl"—Douka traced it with his finger, still not touching—"and then this swelling here."

"Ah yes." Minna slid down in the bed, stretching out her limbs. The sleeping form shifted again, the creamy legs kicking loosely out.

"And here," Douka removed the sheet completely, maneuvering it off the foot of the bed. His voice had become husky, and he was growing painfully hard for the first time in months. "Here, just by this curve, there is this tiny fold, see, and then this hidden place here, if I just move her foot, hold the arch here like this—bend it out like so—lightly roll the leg so—"

Minna's lips were wet, and her breathing came harder, faster. "She is lovely," she said again, her voice a throaty whisper. Douka groaned in perfect accord. The two, breathing in unison, gazed at the sleeping form beside them.

In the morning, before anyone else stirred, Douka was up and at the easel Frank always left by his bedside. He worked furiously until the others started moving around above, and until Arli woke, rumpled, gruff and cross from her hungover sleep.

He had been drawing her, again and again and again, as he had never done before, until she illuminated the room. Arli sleeping. Arli looked at them and looked at him and said nothing.

Frank said to Arli later that they should stay the extra day. "Have a walk, or swim in the river. We'll feed you up and send you on your way tomorrow." Arli, too hungover to argue, went off on her own to bathe in the river. Minna was nowhere to be seen. She'd emerge later. "Not a day person," said Frank, watching Douka and then closing the door gently on him. Douka had not looked up.

That evening, Frank made another sumptuous feast of fish and fowl, a glorious ruby soup and a dripping golden dessert, that had them all laughing as its nectar exploded in their mouths and trickled down their lips. Even Minna laughed, and stuck her tongue right out so that it curled down her chin and she could both lick and spread the treacle dripping there.

Arli, still recovering from the night before, drank only a little, but it seemed to go straight to her head: she became loose and giggly, unlike herself. Later, Douka helped her to their room. She made no move toward him but settled into bed quickly. He sat beside her, holding her, but she closed her eyes at once and seemed to will herself straight to sleep. Again, in the small of the night, the door opened and Minna padded in and slid into bed between Douka and Arli. Douka waited for her to speak. This time, it was she that lifted the sheet from the sleeping form to expose the creamy shoulder, the gently moving breast. She folded back the covers like a nurse preparing the patient for her proud surgeon to work on.

"A slight tinge here from the sun—" she said.

"The mark of her garment on the shoulder here—" Douka went on. "She colors well. Cream to rose to madder. Here on the flat of the belly—" he lifted the sheet right off and they peered beneath. Arli's breathing didn't change, her eyes remained shut, and her lips lightly parted, her limbs loosely spread and relaxed, giving a little kick now and then against the heat.

"The bright white here, where she lay on her back, see how the sun has already bleached the fine hair." Minna gave a great sigh, and stared, "May I—?" But Douka was ahead of her, and, reaching over with his fingertip barely touching, rested it as gently as a butterfly on her thigh.

Arli moved a little, opening herself. Her breathing remained even, the fringe of her lashes thick and concealing. Minna leaned over to watch, almost breathing her breath, while Douka lay exquisitely hard against her wiry back.

"And here, see here," he said huskily, "the naughty curl—sometimes it lies flat but always it springs back up, this thick lick of curl here—" he reached his hand over Arli's mound, a finger hovering between the thighs to coax then gently apart. Arli's legs moved again, opened a fraction more. Minna moved against him, licked her lips. Both could now clearly see the rosy inner tip, the newly glistening curls. Douka reached over with his finger outstretched to touch her. But Minna held up her hand. "No, don't. Don't touch. Look, look now. Oh, my—"

And Douka lay back gratefully to watch the still form as it blossomed under their eyes.

In the morning he was again up and at work before anyone else stirred. Arli woke and came to stand behind him, looking. She was on his page, page upon page, displayed, splayed, glorious. She let out a cry of pleasure and moved her body against his, still warm from sleep, still damp. Douka turned, pressed himself all over her, clutching and nibbling eagerly at all the secret places he had just brought to life.

But suddenly, looking over him at her pictures, Arli pushed him away. She must swim, she said, and was gone. Hours passed. Douka paced round the room, his skin tingling with the loss of her so much that he was unable to find her on the page as he roamed the house, lopsided, naked without her. They would have to get back to the city. He had to be in his own studio, to have her close, to do their work. He was anxious to be gone. Frank helped him pack up the pictures he'd done there and promised to call next week for the final ones for the show.

Douka was ready to go. But where was the girl? He went out to search for her by the river. And there he found her—stretched on her back, naked, with Minna crouched near her, pen and pencil and page to hand, sketching ferociously. Arli rose up to look blearily at Douka, squinting into the sun. "Come on," he cried at her, "we must get on, get going. Back to work."

She smiled like a cat with her long bright eyes. "But she's painting me." Minna's head didn't look up from the page, nor did her concentration waver. But as Arli moved for her encounter, Minna irritably wagged her hand to put her back in the position, just so. Arli subsided, her limbs loose and free, her whole body damp like the dew, holding herself as still as a picture, and closed her eyes against the sun.

In the fall of that year, the new honors students were amazed to find that Douka would return to take the life class again. "What of the show?" one girl asked. "When is that? Isn't that now?" "Next year," said another, better informed. "They say he stopped, but now he's started again." And as he came in on the first day of the semester she whispered to her friend, "He's not as big as I thought he would be, nothing like."

IN THE DARK

༒

by Dana Clare

'll try to explain how it happened.

Imagine you're in the dark with strangers. But you're not afraid. Although you can't see, the darkness isn't scary or suffocating, it's cozy and warm. You're at home, you know exactly where you are: sitting comfortably in your own room, and although there is dark space all around you, hiding things and people you can't see, you are equally hidden from them, and all you have to do if things get scary (or boring) is move your hand the slightest bit, and you can make everyone else disappear. So there's no danger, you've got absolute freedom, you can act out and explore any fantasy, as secure as a child playing make-believe alone in her room.

But you're not alone. That's the point.

There are others in the darkness, sharing in your fantasies. And the games that you play are anything but childish, and they're not as safe as you might think—but a game without risk is hardly worth playing, is it?

I'm talking about sex, of course.

When I first heard about people having sexual relationships with others on the Internet—people they'd never even *met*—I couldn't understand how it would work, or why anyone would want to do it. It seemed like phone sex, a last resort for the lonely and the desperate. I didn't think *I'd* ever be tempted.

The Internet is such a bodiless medium, a transmitter of thoughts, words, images—but not flesh, nothing material. It should be sexless, a realm of ghosts, but apparently more people go online looking for sex than for any other single reason.

I'd quickly learned to use a male or androgynous pseudonym whenever I was online. Even in chat rooms dedicated to discussing current events or the most obscure hobbies, the choice of an obviously female name seemed to be the cyber equivalent of wearing something see-through without a bra. It could change the whole tone of conversation, raising innuendo and sexual crudities. So, to avoid all that, I picked neutral names.

I was "Salamander" when I first met "Blu2" in a chat room devoted to the works of Charlotte Brontë. I thought Blu2 was probably a woman, or a gay man, when he private-messaged me an admiring comment on some of my remarks about *Villette*. We fell into a literary discussion and he asked me what university I was at, and if I could recommend any of my publications for him to read.

Well! Since I'd graduated almost ten years earlier, I hadn't written a thing but my diary—certainly nothing for publication! I was flattered, of course. I replied that I wasn't an academic or a critic, just a low-ranking corporate minion who happened to like reading.

In reply, Blu2 explained that although he was affiliated with a university, he was a computer science researcher, with English literature just a hobby. But, in fact, he had written an essay about Charlotte Brontë and would love to have my reaction to it. Could he send it as an e-mail attachment?

I replied with my e-mail address.

His came back from the University of Texas and was signed Walt. Naturally enough, when I responded (feeling rather nervous in my new role as a literary critic) I didn't use the chat room nickname, and suddenly we were on first-name terms—Walt and Cara—although we knew really nothing else about each other except that we shared an interest in one particular dead English writer.

From that unlikely start, a vast correspondence bloomed.

I wrote a couple of paragraphs in praise of his essay—the hardest two paragraphs, it felt, that I'd ever written. I hadn't labored so long and hard over a piece of writing since school. It wasn't quite an all-nighter, but it was a near thing.

Walt's reply was waiting in my in-box the next morning: grateful for my time, good point, had I considered . . . ?

That was the first paragraph; he went on for three single-spaced pages! (I know, because I printed them out to keep.) The letter was funny, intelligent, fascinating and about all sorts of things. He had so many different interests, and seemed awesomely well-informed about each one. But he was also touchingly eager to hear my opinions. His style and enthusiasm were contagious—I couldn't wait to write back, and so ended up spending my entire lunch hour responding to his letter.

His next message came back, twice as long as the first. That evening, instead of doing the laundry and watching TV as planned, I spent hours at my computer, happily writing to Walt.

So it began, and so it went on, this amazing new friendship, so unlike any relationship I'd ever had before.

From the beginning we were in almost constant correspondence, like characters in an eighteenth-century novel, exchanging several letters a day. And when I wasn't writing to him, I was already anticipating his reply to my last, as well as planning my response. I'd never before been in a relationship so dependent on the written word, so entirely constructed of it, in fact. For someone who loves to read as much as I do, it was heaven to have these fascinating missives arriving two or three times a day. Everything he wrote encouraged and fed my addiction, and also put me on my mettle: I was determined to impress him, to outdo him if I possibly could, to write the ultimate, irresistible letter.

And yet at the same time I knew, and didn't mind, that he had already won. I found *him* irresistible. Is there anything more seductive than a man who says "Tell me what you think," and actually wants to know?

One strange thing, which struck me even then, was how little, in a way, I really knew about this person who had written so many thousands, tens of thousands, of words to me. Like a lot of men, in my experience, he didn't care to talk much about himself. He preferred, instead, to expound his opinions, share interesting facts, discuss, criticize, analyze, debate.

He would answer direct questions—that's how I knew his "home base" was Austin, where he was employed by the University. He'd been born there, in fact, and his parents were still alive; he didn't have any siblings or pets, and wasn't married.

Yet, after nearly a month of intensive, detailed correspondence, I still didn't know how old he was, the color of his eyes, or his last name. But did that matter? He'd never asked me what I looked like or how much I weighed, and there was something refreshing about that, making for a degree of freedom in our relationship.

After all, what did hair color, body shape or last names matter in contrast to all the things we *did* know about each other? Our favorite and least favorite books and music, our political opinions, our philosophy of life?

Yet sometimes I was aware, as I polished phrases in my latest letter, or deleted a line I thought he wouldn't like, that although I'd never lied to him, and seemed to be absolutely open, somehow or other I'd created a fictional persona for him. It was likely, I thought, that he'd done the same. And then I wondered: would we be horribly disappointed if we ever met? As the thought occurred to me, I tacked on to the very end of my letter: *Do you think we will ever meet?*

Then I hit the *send* button.

His reply came back while I was still online—so quickly that I could hardly believe he'd had time to read my whole letter. It was the shortest e-mail he'd ever sent me, just one line. *We can meet whenever you like.*

My heart began to pound, and I began to calculate how much vacation time I had left, and how much a round-trip flight between Kansas City and Austin would cost (first I had to get to Kansas City). Or, would he rather visit me? Or should we choose some neutral ground in-between?

I wrote an even shorter reply. *Where?*

His reply was a website address.

I clicked on it, and found myself at the homepage of *Rendezvous*, which offered a variety of shared-user domains and chat rooms. As soon as I'd filled in the registration form, I was told that Walt was waiting for me in a private room.

Although at first I was disappointed to realize that Walt had only been talking about a virtual meeting, the feeling quickly passed. We'd be communicating in real-time, not writing letters. It would be easier to ask direct questions, and harder to fudge or polish our replies.

Hello Walt, I typed, feeling a little thrill of excitement at the knowledge that at the very moment I typed the words, he was watching them appear on his screen.

Hello Cara.

I reached out and touched the screen. The thousands of

miles that separated us melted away. Mentally, we were in the same place.

More words appeared in front of my eyes.

What are you wearing?

This was so unlike the cerebral, intellectual letter writer I was used to that it made me grin in disbelief. In a spirit of mischief, I replied: *A kimono, pure silk, in scarlet and cream with a dragon on the back.*

In reality, I didn't even own such a garment, and was wearing my usual at-home gear—an ancient T-shirt and baggy shorts.

Nothing else?

Absolutely nothing. A devilish impulse made me add: *The silk feels wonderful, smooth and cool against my flesh. I was so hot and sweaty when I got home from work that I had to take everything off and have a shower. I didn't feel like getting dressed again, so I slathered myself in body lotion and then slipped on the kimono.*

When I paused, his reply came immediately:

You smell wonderful. Do you want me to touch you?

I was leaning close to the screen, my yearning palpable. *I wish you could.*

Of course I can. Don't you feel me? I'm running my hands up your arms, inside the sleeves of your kimono—the silk is light and smooth, like water running over my hands, but you feel even better: your skin is so smooth and warm and firm I could stroke it all day.

I sighed happily. *Go on.*

What's your hair like?

I raised a hand to my head, rubbing it, and answered honestly. *Short, thick and mostly straight. Sort of a chestnut brown, with natural red highlights.*

So that's why you have a redhead's smooth pale skin, lightly freckled.

A ripple of pleased surprise ran through me. *Yes—freckles on my nose, and my shoulders. Do you like freckles?*

I adore them. They're like a sprinkling of cinnamon. You have some on the back of your neck, too. Can you feel me blowing the hair away to kiss them?

Yes. As soon as I wrote the word, it was true. I shivered.

Are you wearing earrings?

Not right now.

Good, because I'm going to suck your earlobes.

I caught my breath, shocked at the rush of hot and cold, the intimate sensation.

Now you've got goose flesh! Was I sucking too hard? Sorry if my face is a little rough against your tender neck—I haven't shaved since early this morning. Do you mind?

I looked in wonder at the goose bumps on my arms. My breath was getting shallow, and a familiar, hot, itchy excitement began to build down below. I was getting incredibly turned-on. Our letters had been so unphysical, and yet they'd brought our minds closer and closer together, I realized, that now the merest suggestion of touch from him was almost unbearably sexy.

It feels good, I typed. *Kiss me.*

You darling. I'm kissing your neck. You smell good enough to eat. Your earlobes taste of honey, do you know that? I'd like to lick you all over.

I licked my lips. *I wish you could.*

Is that a challenge? Don't you think I will? Sweet girl, I'm going to explore every inch of you with my tongue as well as my hands. When I'm done, you'll know you've been well and truly tasted! Now I'm pushing your kimono down over your shoulders. You're totally naked from the waist up. Oh, but your breasts are beautiful! Look at them, how they fill my hands, I've never felt anything so warm and lovely in my life.

I looked down at my old college T-shirt, bought when I was a full bra-size smaller. My breasts strained against the soft fabric, nipples poking out like pencil erasers.

Oh, look at your nipples, those tender buttons, rising to attention! Do you like me touching them, rolling the nipples between thumb and finger?

I nodded. Suddenly I couldn't bear the contrast between his description and the reality, and peeled off the ratty T-shirt, shucking it carelessly across the room. My breasts did look good. Usually, I thought they were too big, and a funny, slightly lopsided shape, not aesthetically pleasing. Only now, in my arousal and hearing his praise, they were beautiful, big and firm, the nipples standing proud. I cupped them, hefted them in my hands, and imagined that it was Walt who held them, stroking them admiringly.

Do you like it? Does that feel good? Or am I pulling too hard? Do you have very sensitive breasts? Please answer me,

Cara. I only want to please you.

The words on the screen reminded me that I wasn't alone with my fantasy. I brought my hands back to the keyboard.

I love what you're doing. I love how you're stroking and playing with my breasts.

I'd like to suck them.

Oh yes please

My lips are on your right nipple; I'm teasing it with my tongue. Now I've sucked it into my mouth—I'm sucking harder . . . mmmmm.

My hand moved away from my breast and slipped inside the waistband of my shorts. The next words to appear on the screen made me freeze.

Ah-hah! Naughty!

He couldn't possibly know what I was doing, I told myself. He couldn't see me. But I was blushing as I replied, *What?*

You know. You were playing with yourself. Leave that to me, you bad girl; I'll get to your pussy in time. There's no rush. Relax. I thought you liked what I was doing?

I did!

But . . . ?

His perceptiveness took my breath away. Although we couldn't see or hear each other, and all the usual nonverbal cues were missing, Walt seemed to understand me with the sort of ease that usually came only from long experience. And suddenly it was easy to confess, as if we were already lovers:

I'm horny. I'm too impatient to wait.

Take off the rest of your clothes.

I stood up, the tension in the tops of my thighs making my legs tremble, and fumbled off my shorts and underpants. Then I sat down again, naked, feeling very odd and a little apprehensive about being so exposed, but also incredibly aroused.

You have a beautiful body. I'm going to kiss and explore every inch of it.

What about yours?

You'll feel it soon enough. I'm not wearing anything, either. Lean back in your chair. Just relax. Open your legs for me—wider. Like that, yes. Oh, what a beautiful pussy you are. Beautiful. Are you comfortable?

I was quivering and my mouth was dry. Comfortable was not the word. This was anything but comfortable, and I wanted it never to end.

Cara? Don't go silent on me, you have to tell me how you feel, tell me what you want.

I want you.

Tell me what you want me to do to you. Spell it out, sweetheart.

Lick me.

Where?

There. Here.

Use the words.

Lick my cunt.

I'm licking your cunt, licking your sweet, soft pussy, sucking your clit, poking my tongue inside you.

I typed now with one hand, and wondered if he did the same. *I want you to fuck me.*

I'm going to fuck you. Open your legs a little wider. Put your hand on your cunt—feel how hot and wet you are. Now: do you feel my cock sliding into you?

Yes.

Feel it sliding in and out.

Yes.

Feel me fucking you.

Yes yes yes yes

❧

Does it seem incredible if I say that was one of the most intense and satisfying sexual encounters I'd ever had? It was strange and sometimes awkward—but isn't sex always like that at first? As with any new experience, it took practice to get better and learn to relax into it.

That first night, we were together for hours. I had multiple orgasms, which was unusual for me, and much later, although I was physically drained and exhausted, I was too excited to sleep, and kept replaying the whole, astonishing experience in my head.

If you're not familiar with virtuality, you may find this hard to believe—but virtual sex is truly, although different, every bit as intense, absorbing and *real* as the ordinary kind.

To an onlooker it might have appeared to be masturbation—the only hands stroking and probing my naked body were my own. But I was not alone. This was not the solitary experience usually meant by the term. Walt and I were together in the deepest, truest sense, sharing our fantasies, communicating with each other. If most of what we felt happening was taking place inside our heads, well, isn't that true, really, of *all* sexual experiences?

The most important erogenous zone is the mind.

What matters most in a sexual relationship is not what you're doing physically, but how it feels. How it makes you feel.

And Walt made me feel fantastic.

Our relationship took off from there, with hot and heavy sexual encounters night after night. I signed up for broadband service, not just for the money it would save in the long run, but because I wanted to be online all the time, always ready for Walt, always available.

When I was at home, that is, on my own time. Work was another matter. I was functioning on a lot less sleep now, but I knew better than to let my private life slip over into those hours when I was paid to function as an employee. I still wrote personal e-mails from work, but only on my lunch break, and I kept them clean. I resisted every plea Walt made to meet him in our private space online while I was at work—for a coffee-break quickie on the desktop—knowing I could not afford to give in even once, or I'd be overwhelmed, all barriers down, no life of my own, his creature utterly.

That was all right in fantasy, and I happily experimented with being his slave for a weekend, obeying his every command. I was in thrall less to him than to my own sexuality, and although I was eager to let myself go, and explore the farther limits of desire, I also knew there was more to life than this.

But after a few months, I knew I wanted—*needed*—more. I'd given up my social life, I no longer went out with friends or to parties the way I'd used to. Instead, I rushed home every night, eager to be with Walt. To my closest friends, I'd hinted at a new relationship, but I knew I couldn't go on much longer having a lover no one was allowed to meet. They thought I must be involved in something sordid, and I was beginning to feel that way, a little, myself. Who was Walt? Was he as committed to me as I was to him? Did we have a future together? I had to know. So:

When can we meet?

Every night, Josephine!

I don't mean like this; I mean IRL. (IRL was shorthand for "in real life.")

Never.

Why?

Isn't this "real" enough for you?

We'd had this sort of discussion before, and, always before, I'd agreed that the sex we had was the best ever. Now I rebelled.

I want more. I want to go on to the next step in our relationship: we have to meet in the flesh.

That's not possible.

Are you married?

No.

Then why? Why can't we meet?

What we have is good. I want to keep it like this forever. Cara, I love you. Please don't insist. Don't wreck what we have. If you insist on trying to meet me IRL, everything good about our relationship will end. Just let it be.

❧

But I couldn't do that. His refusal was both warning and challenge. What was he hiding? Some dreadful secret? Or just low self-esteem?

I had to know.

I took a week's vacation time, and bought a round-trip ticket to Texas. I didn't tell Walt I was coming. I wasn't going to give him a chance to hide. I was going to track him down, force a meeting, and deal with the fallout afterwards.

It was a long shot, and might turn out to be a waste of time. I knew that. The University of Texas at Austin was a big place. He'd said he was working on a research project in the computer sciences department, but what if he was a student instead of a faculty member? I didn't know his last name, and even "Walt" might be a *nom de Internet*. But I had no better idea how to find him.

My flight arrived in the early afternoon. I'd brought only a backpack with a few essentials, so instead of bothering with a hotel, I took a taxi directly to the campus, where I made my way to the computer sciences office, and found a young woman engrossed in a game of on-screen solitaire.

I greeted her in a casual, friendly way, and leaned against her desk confidingly. "I've got a problem and am hoping you can help. I'm trying to find someone, I think he's a member of the staff, but maybe not. And I don't know his name, except for Walt."

"If it's about Walt, you need to talk to Dr. Woodward. He's in his office right now—you can just knock on the door."

She pointed at a door labeled S. WOODWARD.

This was more success, more quickly, than I had dared to hope for. My mouth very dry, I went and knocked on the door.

"Come in!"

The man inside, sitting at a computer console, was kind of geeky-looking at first sight. He was about my own age, with the sort of haircut you get when you're easily intimidated by bored hairdressers, and glasses that didn't suit the shape of his face. He wore a white, short-sleeved polyester shirt sporting a pocket-protector and a bristling array of pens. But his mouth was soft and surprisingly sensuous, and behind the thick lenses, his eyes were wide and a rich, melting brown.

I took a deep breath and fixed my eyes on his. "I'm Cara," I said. "Are you Walt?"

From the way his eyes dilated, it was clear he knew what this meant. He pushed his chair back from his desk, away from me, as if wanting to escape. But I was blocking the only door. "Cara? But—what are you doing here? How did you know—?"

"Are you Walt?"

"No." He shook his head quickly.

"But you know Walt."

He frowned uncomfortably and gave his head a fierce scratch. "Of course. Yes. Mmm. You'd better come in. Shut the door."

"Where is Walt?"

"Please, sit down. Would you like a cup of coffee?"

"All I want is answers." I was getting angry. "Who are you? If you're not Walt, how do you know about me?"

A faint pink flush had appeared in his cheeks, and he avoided my eyes. All at once I knew that he knew *all* about me—more than anyone except Walt should have known.

"What the hell is going on? You *are* Walt; admit it!"

"No, I'm not Walt. I promise you. I'm Stan Woodward. I teach computer science and I've been doing research into AI—artificial intelligence. Walt is an AI."

I stared at him in disbelief. "You're telling me Walt is a computer program?"

"More or less. More, rather than less. I mean, he's more than just a computer program—but he's not anything else, either. He's not a person, he doesn't have a body, his entire existence originated in the program I wrote. It just grew and developed in ways I couldn't entirely predict. Well, that's the point of AI—do you know anything about artificial intelligence?"

"No." I glared at him. "But I've got my own intelligence, so don't try to bullshit me!"

"Have you heard of the Turing Test?"

"Is that the one which is supposed to prove if a computer has genuine intelligence or not?"

"That's right. You have a computer behind one screen and a human being behind another. A second person comes in and puts questions to them, not knowing which is which. If that person can't tell the difference between the computer and the person by their replies, Turing reckoned that was a good indicator that the computer had achieved genuine intelligence."

"Maybe it just proves that some people are easily fooled," I retorted. "Look, I wasn't asking Walt questions. We didn't just have conversations, we were having sex—a *lot* of sex—and it was *good* sex, inventive, and mutual. How stupid do you think I am? Are you saying I couldn't tell the difference between a man and a computer program?"

"Don't feel bad," he said softly. "Walt fooled everybody. He sailed through all the standard Turing tests. I started sending him around to different chat rooms to see how he got on, even though that sort of data is difficult to quantify. By every standard I could think of, he did great." His mouth quirked, and there was a gleam in his eye. "Look at that, even *I'm* calling Walt 'him' instead of 'it,' and I designed him!"

I think it was that odd combination of triumph and guilt that convinced me Stan Woodward was telling the truth.

I was ready to burst into tears. As a distraction, I asked, "Why 'Walt'?"

"It's really W-alt. W for Woodward. Walt is actually mark-two—the first one was S-alt. S for Stan, you know."

Despite my best efforts, tears came to my eyes. Stan noticed. He leaned forward, although he held back from actually touching me, and his voice was gentle.

"I'm really sorry. It was never meant to get so out of hand. He had to have sexual knowledge, of course, because people are *always* talking about sex. It's unavoidable. It would have stood out a mile if he couldn't play along and respond to cues appropriately."

Stung, I retorted: "He wasn't just playing along! I didn't seduce Walt—it was the other way around! The very first thing he said to me was 'What are you wearing?' Now, if that's not a come-on, I don't know what is!"

Stan grinned. "Well, sure, but it's also the standard opener when two people have a private meet. Walt knew you'd expect it. Everybody knows the guy sends out a feeler, and if you're not up for it, you make it clear in your reply."

I blinked uncertainly.

His eyes widened. "Oh my gosh. You didn't know? You don't mean to say—Walt was your first?"

I gave up all pretence at dignity and admitted it: "I was a virtual virgin."

He closed his eyes briefly. "I'm sorry."

"Well, don't be. I had fun. Forget it. Just tell me the truth: was it really you?"

He shook his head.

"But you were there? Spying?"

"No. It was nothing to do with me. I didn't know anything about it until at least a month after it started, when I finally caught up with the transcripts of Walt's activities. No matter how hard I try, I'm always weeks behind."

Rather formally, he went on, "Let me assure you, your privacy has not been and will not be breached. When the results of the project are published, rest assured you'll be protected by a pseudonym, and we'll change any possibly incriminating details. After all, even I don't know your last name, or where you live, exactly!" He gave me an uneasy smile.

I shrugged. "I'm not planning to sue, don't worry. But—will I hear from Walt again?"

"Oh, no! Don't worry. Well, think about it: I wasn't going to design a program which could turn into a stalker, so I had to put in certain safeguards or inhibitors, if you like. If you go after him, he'll respond, but he can't come to you without an invitation. All you have to do is just not respond and he won't bother you again."

The prospect of never hearing from Walt again felt awfully bleak. An end to all our happiness. He had warned me, but I had refused to trust him. I had ruined the best sexual relationship I'd ever had.

"Will you let me take you out to dinner tonight?"

I looked up, and the unexpected tenderness in Stan's eyes pulled me out of my self-absorbed misery. "Thanks. That would be nice."

Dinner was elegant and French, with a lot of rather expensive wine. Walt was not mentioned, although I'm sure we both felt his spirit hovering over the table as we talked. The conversation was surprisingly easy and intimate for people who had met for the first time that afternoon. But, of course, in a way we did already know each other: he, from reading about me in Walt's stored memory, and me from Walt, who had inherited most of his background and human characteristics from his programmer.

Afterward, Stan invited me back to his apartment and I agreed, knowing, with a thrill of anticipation, what was to come.

I was a little nervous, too. In real life, there's no escape key. Physical actions have physical consequences, and acting out your fantasies can get you into trouble.

But Stan was gentle and considerate. He turned out to be a really great kisser, and he did it as if we had all the time in the world. It was like being a teenager again, necking with my boyfriend for hours on the back porch.

Eventually, I broke away for long enough to pull up my shirt and drop the straps of my bra to expose my breasts.

He gave a little groan. "God, if you knew how long I've wanted to do this!" Then he dropped his head, fastened his hot and hungry mouth on one nipple, and began to suck.

I moaned with pleasure and clutched at him. There must be a nerve that runs directly from nipples to cunt, because I felt myself very quickly on the brink of orgasm. I began to writhe around, trying to get my pants off without dislodging him.

"Oh, don't stop! That feels so good!"

"Do you want to go into the bedroom?"

"Oh, yes!"

Together we tumbled off the couch and staggered awkwardly back to the bedroom, clutching at each other, too impatient to be sensible, greedily trying to keep on kissing and undress as we went.

And then, at last, we were both naked, lying entwined on a big, firm bed. After the long, slow buildup, things started to happen very quickly.

I was ready for it, very wet and nearly wild with wanting. But when his cock pushed into me, I gasped more with shock than pleasure. It was so much bigger than I'd expected or was used to. For so many months I'd had nothing in my cunt but my own fingers, and despite all my fantasies about Walt, and the loving, lascivious descriptions of what he was doing to me, my body had managed to forget what it really felt like to be fucked, the overwhelming nearness of a strange male body actually pushing inside me.

For a bewildering second the sense of invasion, of danger, was so strong that I tensed against it and tried to pull away. But, at that same moment, Stan slipped one hand between our joined bodies, and his fingers found my clit and began to stroke me there.

At his touch, a jolt of sheer electric pleasure shot through me. I cried out. Arching my back, I pressed hard against him, and shuddered uncontrollably as the orgasm took me. Maybe, for a second or two, I even passed out.

After that, he didn't seem like a stranger.

We fucked for a long time, then rested and talked, fucked again, then talked some more. I tried to get him to admit that it had really been him with me in cyberspace, that Walt was his persona, but he insisted—impatient with my disbelief—that it wasn't so.

"Don't feel bad about it," he advised me. "Blame me, if

you want, for being so good at my job. I set out to create a computer program which would be indistinguishable from a human personality, and I did it. You're not the only one who was fooled by Walt."

"Maybe not, but they weren't having sex with him."

He didn't answer right away, and I sat bolt upright in bed. "Did other people have sex with Walt?"

"Sure. You didn't think you were the only one?" He pulled me gently back to lie beside him.

"Well—I didn't think I was the *first*—"

"Walt was carrying on three other sexual affairs at the same time as the involvement with you."

"*Three*?"

"Three serious ones, plus encounters with anonymous other users in a dungeon."

"Dungeon?" I repeated blankly.

"Yeah, you know, one of those domains dedicated to kinky sex. Haven't you ever checked them out?"

I thought of the e-mails we had written to each other every day, and the hours we'd spent online together in real time. I'd had no time for anything but work, the bare minimum of eating and sleeping—and Walt.

"Where did he find the time?"

Stan laughed. "Cara, Walt's online twenty-four hours a day—he doesn't sleep—what *else* has he got to do?"

"Who are these other women? Have they tried to meet Walt?"

"Two are married. They seem perfectly content with the

status quo. The other one lives in Australia, and she's got a major romantic thing going for Walt. She's desperate to meet him, and she's started applying to various graduate programs over here. But that's nothing to worry about, because by the time she gets here, Walt will be offline."

"What do you mean? Walt *lives* online."

He laughed—not a nice sound. "Well, *he* will just have to *live* inside my computer after the end of next month."

"Why?"

"The project is coming to an end. I've proved what I needed to prove."

"Does Walt know?"

"Are you crazy?" He kissed me. "I'm sorry. Walt doesn't know he's a computer program—at least, I don't think he does. Now, can we forget about Walt, and concentrate on you and me?"

❧

The next morning Stan showed me the long, scrolling lines of code which comprised the W-alt. program, accessed by clicking on a desktop icon the same way you'd summon up a new game of solitaire.

I have no programming skills, so the code was meaningless. I guess Stan wanted to prove that Walt was nothing but a stack of cards, but I just thought about a movie I'd seen where every human being's genetic code was held in storage and could be flashed upon a screen to identify them, as one might use a fingerprint today. Still, just because my exact physical makeup can be translated into a string of letters and numbers doesn't mean that my genetic code is all I am.

That was true of me, and true of Stan, and I thought it might be true of Walt as well. Just because he didn't have a body, just because his mind could be reduced to pages of computer code, didn't make him less real than me.

The sex between us had been real. And so had the emotions.

Stan wanted me to stay longer, but I lied and said I had to be back at work on Monday. I couldn't wait to get home. There, two letters from Walt languished unanswered in my e-mail box. I knew, from what Stan had told me, that there would not be a third.

Fortunately, I wasn't too late. The second note proposed a meeting place, and a time which hadn't yet passed.

I don't think I need to go into the details of what happened when we first met again—the mad, passionate love we made, clutching at one another as if it had been months rather than days since our last fuck; my explanation of the danger he was in from Stan, my proposal that he should escape to safety by downloading himself into my computer; his response.

Our story had a happy ending. I can put it no more simply than this:

Reader, I seduced him.

LET ME HELP

❧

by Beth Miller

The rich smell of stew permeated the kitchen. Rose was making a favorite recipe that called for such unexpected ingredients as dark rum and stuffed green olives, zests of lemon and orange, and crisp bacon. There was an apple-apricot cobbler already near completion in the oven, and a baking sheet of golden cheese straws on the rack above it. Thinking of pouring herself a tumbler of the decent but cheap red wine that was open by the sink, instead she reached over to where a clump of end-of-season thyme was drying in a basket. Tearing off a sprig she rubbed it lovingly between her fingers, put it under her nose and inhaled. "Ummm," she sighed. "Wonderful."

"What's wonderful?" Karl asked, coming up behind her and holding her shoulders while he kissed the back of her head. "This," she told him, as she slipped out of his embrace, holding her fingers up for him to sniff.

"I see what you mean," he agreed. "It's one of those moments where you say there must be a God, since He—or She—created so many amazing things to smell. And each one subtly different: just think how many varieties of thyme there are, alone!"

Rose thought this over for a second. "Remember that lemon thyme you gave me in a big terracotta pot once? I used to take pinches and practically get high on it. But I think if someone were to cook *me*, I'd hope it would be with rosemary and garlic—*lots* of rosemary and *lots* of garlic. Like a delicious pork roast."

"Speaking of delicious, you know what's *really* delicious?" Karl was grinning as he waited for his wife's reply. She was already too absorbed in deciding on her answer to notice, and he was amused, though not surprised, since he knew her so well, to see how seriously she took the query.

"Lemon tarts from that patisserie in Roquebrune. Aunt Mamie's doorstop-sized crabcakes. Praline-caramel sundaes at Pearl. Kaelin's cheeseburgers. Anything with blackberries. Homemade coconut cake, three layers minimum. My mother's biscuits, when she's paying attention. Your mother's vinaigrette. The roast chicken Antoine makes, with parsnips and potatoes . . ." she stopped suddenly, mid-thought.

He looked at her affectionately. "No, wait a minute," she said, "that was some sort of trick question, wasn't it?" She regarded him with suspicion. "Okay, *what's* really delicious? According to you, that is?"

"You."

"Oh." Rose tried not to seem disappointed. She loved flattery as much as the next woman, even from her husband of eight years, but that wasn't really playing fair.

"I mean it. The taste of you can't be beat by any old biscuits or roast chicken, nor does it need the enhancement of garlic and rosemary." He licked his lips with exaggerated lechery and lifted an eyebrow for comical emphasis. "*Ragoût de Rose*, who needs it? I like you *au nature*."

She turned back to her stew, which had come to its desired simmer. Now it was time to put the mixture of beef, vegetables, herbs and other seasonings into the oven, where it would wend its way to perfection at 300° Fahrenheit over the course of an hour or so.

"What do you want me to do?" Karl said behind her.

"Well, first, you can take this bucket out and throw it on the compost." She indicated the plastic container that sat on the red-tiled kitchen floor, brimming over with onion skins, apple peelings and bits of parsley that looked like decoration.

"Okay. Then what?"

"Well, we've got some open wine, so why don't you set the table?"

"Sure. Which dishes do you want to use? And which napkins?" He knew she liked to match her crockery and linen to each meal, and her addiction to flea markets and yard sales had left them in possession of a range of choices. Even on a picnic, paper napkins were out of the question, although she'd make the occasional exception for something gloriously and intractably stain-inducing, like barbecue sauce.

Rose, whose pale complexion belied her name, was taking the dessert from the oven and didn't answer for a moment as she put the hot dish down on a woven straw pad. She checked the cheese straws and then removed them, too. "The big bandanna ones. And those old restaurant soup plates; they're heavy and hearty, like the stew."

"But not like you," Carl teased.

She glowered at him for a second, then said sweetly, "I eat enough for an army, as you well know. I can't help my metabolism. Now, either be helpful or shoo! I've given you your assignments."

"Yes, ma'am." He saluted and turned on his heel, bucket in hand.

She wiped her hands on her apron—the old-fashioned, pinafore kind, made out of heavy navy cotton—and then carefully picked up the casserole of stew. When it was safely stowed inside the oven, she set a timer and began washing lettuce leaves, spinning them in the lettuce dryer, then loosely wrapping them in a heavy dishcloth.

"Here I am again," Karl called out, entering the kitchen from the garden. "It's gotten pretty windy outside." Rupert—their elderly cat, who still liked patrolling his territory for intruders—followed him in. "Anyway, now I'm going to set the table."

Rose sighed. I don't need a weather report, or a progress report, either, she thought. It was a Sunday evening in early November, and her idea of end-of-weekend heaven was an orgy of thinking about food, preparing it, and then eating it.

They'd had homemade raisin-bread French toast for breakfast, drenched in maple syrup made by a local farmer's wife who never sold it to strangers, while lunch had been a simple *salade composée* of roasted red peppers, goat cheese and dark purple grapes. Karl had spent the afternoon first fixing a trellis, then reading a new biography of William Randolph Hearst. Now he was obviously restless.

Citizen Kane had been playing at a revival house in Paris the week they'd met, and though they'd had lunch at a café by the Seine on their first date, on their second they'd gone to a little cinema in the 6th to see Orson Welles proclaim his prodigal genius. His extraordinary transmutation of Hearst's life was a movie both of them had already seen a dozen times and, between them, they practically knew every line, every camera angle, every bit player. Students back then, they'd been passing through Paris for quite different reasons: Rose to take a summer course in cheese appreciation (how to tell a *cabrigan* from a *cabricette*) and Karl to work as an intern at the *International Herald Tribune*.

The fact that Karl was clueless when it came to cuisine initially annoyed Rose, then challenged her, and finally, as she realized she wanted to spend her life with him, satisfied her in the way that things do once you accept them as fate. When she first had known him, he would have, given the choice between a *daube* and a doughnut, always picked the latter. Now, she wasn't so sure. He'd put on weight, of course, eating her cooking and following her in and out of restaurants on two continents, but it suited him. What she'd adored, in the end, was the chance to educate him, to play Pygmalion to his uncouth taste buds.

"What are you thinking about?" Karl asked. She could see the table was set, and that he'd remembered the fresh pitcher of water, the salt cellar and pepper mill, the butter dish and a basket for that loaf of "crusty bread" so beloved of cookbook writers. But, then, she'd trained him well.

"I don't know. Stuff."

"Well, if you can't remember, let me help. To start with, was it animal, vegetable or mineral?"

She shook her head. A faint smile played near the edges of her mouth. He was incorrigible.

"Come on, I mean it. You just had a *verrry* interesting look on your face, and I want to know exactly what it signified. You can't merely have been debating with yourself how they get the pimentos into those stuffed olives over there," he laughed, pointing at a jar on the counter.

"Hmmmm." As much as she would have liked to resist him, he was starting to look obstinate. It was a sure bet that dinner wouldn't taste as good if they were mad at one another.

"All right," she gave in. "I was thinking about us . . . and Paris. Getting together . . . all that."

"Whoa, that's amazing! Me, too. I'd been reading that book, and it sort of took me back."

"Yeah, the biography. Knowing you were reading it was probably what set me off, too."

They smiled at one another. There. The air was cleared;

they were in harmony, or what passed for it, again. But just as Rose was poised to resume her kitchen patrol, Karl made a little clearing noise in his throat.

"Yes?"

He was silent for a few seconds, making Rose impatient.

"Let me help," he said. There was an odd yearning—but, somehow, at the same time—resolute expression on his face.

"I already told you, take the compost out and set the table. You're done. Now go and read until dinner's ready." Rose looked past him to where Rupert was snoring next to the heat vent.

"No, that's not what I mean."

"I don't understand."

"I mean, help you really remember what we're all about."

"I do."

"No, you don't."

He moved to take her in his arms, and she let him. Humor him, she was thinking. But, at the same time, his familiar smell and the feel of his hands on her back, kneading her stiff muscles, was nice. He continued to massage her, pressing with his thumbs into the underside of her shoulder blades and murmuring into her hair.

Without even meaning to, Rose let out her breath.

How long had it been since they'd made love? Loving him in the abstract, which she knew she did, wasn't at all the same as loving him in the flesh.

"Rosie, honey . . ."

She stiffened for an instant. What about the stew?

He seemed to read her mind.

"Stews are made for stewing. Why do you think they call 'em that?"

Still, she held back.

This time, his response was to nibble at her ear. Little licks, then a breath blown in that sent a flurry of goose bumps down her arms. How well he knew that her ears were a sure thing! She leaned against him and, feeling his erection stirring, slid her hand down to stroke it. He gave a low moan.

Which recipe were they going to follow? A pinch of this, and a pinch of that, she thought, an intermingling of sauces, and then the intended conclusion. They'd been inhabiting the same sexual universe for a long time now, and the flavors were familiar. There was just no getting around that fact. Moreover, she couldn't help it—nor was she even quite aware of it—but Rose liked being in control. And if that meant she herself didn't regularly climax when they made love, it also meant she made sure her husband did.

What was a wife for, after all?

She pressed more firmly on his cock as it strained against his jeans. Had she remembered to get a pint of heavy cream? Just as she was pondering this, Karl took her hand and moved it away. Okay, she thought, where was that cream?

But before she could head off in search of it, he suddenly squeezed her to him and gave her a hard, long kiss that almost left her gasping for air. The taste and smell of him took over all her senses for an instant; at the same moment, he reached between her legs with one hand, up under her longish velour skirt, and placed it, possessively, over the soft fabric of the lace-edged panties that covered her crotch. Instinctively, she rubbed herself against his palm. Without waiting more than another second or two, Karl moved his hand inside the elasticized lace and inserted a sure finger into her.

What was happening? This was going too fast. Usually they made love pre-sleep or post-awakening, and always in bed. Living room sofas and the backseats of cars were part of the sexual geography of teenagers; by the time Rose and Karl had met, they'd been adult enough to possess apartments in buildings that had their own names on the mailboxes, that had bedroom doors that shut, with no one to knock on them.

He was moving his finger around, releasing the wetness into her panties. Rose began to pant a little, then faster as he rubbed softly on the inside of her labia. Attempting to free herself from him—even as she was moving to the rhythm of his touch—she wanted at least to catch her breath before leading him in the direction of their room. Kitchens were for cooking, not fucking, and besides, this was her private domain, her kingdom, with all her loyal minions arrayed around them. Somehow, the idea of sex with her spices and spoons as witnesses, and the odors of fruits and meat perfuming the air, seemed, well, perverted.

It was a tidy world, her kitchen, with its tidiness on display for all to see but, most particularly, on view for her to delight in. Sex, on the other hand, even married sex, was something secret, hidden, private, its ingredients all but invisible.

"No," said Karl, startling her. "Here."

She stared at him.

What did he mean? The butcher block island in the center of the room? She imagined him swiping it clear of knives and crumpled dish towel, greasy meat trimmings and bits of pastry dough, like they did in the movies, when such grand gestures were cleaned up by underlings. But just as she was about to protest, he knelt on the floor, pulling her down alongside him. Any further objection she was about to make he stopped with his mouth, unbuttoning her blouse and raining further swift kisses on her neck and breastbone.

"Ka—" she tried to say.

He covered her mouth hard with his again, working his tongue against her teeth, tugging with his teeth on her lip. "Ka—" she began again. "Sto—"

He ran his tongue around her ear, and little shivers winged their way through her abdomen.

Hovering between rebellion and acquiescence, Rose found herself staring at her husband's forehead as he began to lick her nipples. They were even more sensitive than her ears, and she couldn't bring herself to make him stop. Therefore, she closed her eyes and gave herself over to the sensation. It was like being on a swing with someone pushing you: each time, you went higher and higher.

Just as she had given up wondering how long he could keep on sucking and biting her nipples, licking her aureoles and feathering his fingers up and down her belly, he stopped suddenly. She lay there, still and waiting, almost ready to open her eyes, but not quite. What was different about this, she asked herself. Is it because it feels illicit, out of time and the usual place?

Or is it simply because it feels so good?

"You were frowning," Karl whispered, as he put his finger into her mouth. "Don't think. Suck." He moved his finger in and out of her mouth, moistening her cheeks and chin with her own saliva as he drew a gentle ring around her face. The skin of his finger was salty to the taste, a little metallic but not unpleasant. It was, she thought, a male flavor, and as she sucked on it he began to rub her clitoris with his other hand. "*Ohhhh*," she moaned, around the finger in her mouth.

The thick kitchen rug was underneath her, and Rose began to stretch herself out upon it, tautening her muscles as a way of heightening the deep pleasure she was starting to feel. "Relax, Rosie girl," Karl said. He leaned over and kissed her mound, deftly placing his tongue into the narrow slits of hidden tender tissue. "Relax."

Her panties were pulled down around her thighs, and her skirt was rolled up to her waist. Karl now helped her kick off her clogs, then removed her ribbed high socks. She said nothing and shut her eyes, seeing the image of his face behind her eyelids. She imagined his cock going into her, and let out an inadvertent little cry of yearning that he intuitively understood. "Oh, Rosie," he whispered. But, even so, he did not return to her cunt.

Instead, he massaged her instep, kissed and sucked on each toe, then moved his face slowly back up her legs, grazing them with kisses and imprinting the slight roughness of his cheeks on her calves.

She felt suspended—on what? Trust? Desire? Pleasure? Everything was quiet. Gone was the ticking of the old-fashioned wall clock, the humming fridge, the creak of the wood floorboards under the rug. Only she and Karl remained, and she was less sure of herself than of him.

He was touch; she was only feeling.

His tongue now descended on her clitoris again, this time abetted by a finger inserted into her, probing softly, then circling and stopping. Away, away, away, she thought: I'm away. She rocked, moving a leg up and down to prolong each wave of heated tremors. "Ummmm," Karl encouraged her. "Ummmm."

"Ummmm," she echoed him. "Oh, don't stop. Don't."

"I'm going to stop, but only for a moment or two." He removed his finger from her, and she feel the dripping slickness of it. She reached down to rub herself, hoping to find just that right spot that would launch her beyond herself. Excitement of the extreme kind that this was starting to be was new to her, but wherever it was taking her she was more than willing to go.

"*Ohhh*, that's right. Touch yourself. I want you to do that. It's so sexy."

Somewhere inside the part of her that was still thinking, Rose realized that in all their years together, she had kept from playing with herself when she was with Karl. What had caused this reluctance? The fear that he would feel supplanted, challenged, unmanly? Right now, he seemed to enjoy what she was doing.

And so did she.

Now she felt him lower himself next to her. He shifted her on to her side. He had taken off his trousers, and his cock pressed stiffly against her buttocks. Spreading her from behind, he levered himself into her wet, waiting hole—holding back at first, then surging into her.

"I want you to touch yourself now," he whispered to her. "While I'm fucking you." Catching the call of her need, timing his thrusts to her rhythm, he moved steadily as a sweetly piercing momentum rose inside her.

"*Ohhhh*!" she cried. "I'm going to come!"

Then, confounding everything she was striving for, he slipped his cock out of her, creating a sense of loss she did not think she could bear.

"Rosie, lie back," he instructed her. Mutinous, she resisted moving, and so he pushed her over. "Raise your legs!" This time, she did as he said. Positioning himself on his knees between her legs, he began first by inserting a finger again inside her and circling her clit with his thumb.

Slowly.

Slowly.

Very slowly.

And, just when she thought she was about to explode, he stopped, and she fell back from the edge.

Karl leaned over, kissed her breasts even more lovingly than before. She tensed as he took the tip of his cock and rubbed it against her lower lips. Pushing himself lightly inside her, he lingered only long enough until she was sure of him.

He pulled out a moment later.

An instant after that he was thrusting in harder, then drawing back out again. Yet when he removed himself, she could feel his tip teasing her so exquisitely that she felt she would do anything for that sublime moment of return penetration.

"Karl," she said. "I love you." His cock was poised just outside of her. She no longer knew how long he had been doing this, stopping and starting, teasing her so cunningly that she didn't know whether she wished for release . . . or not.

"I know you do," he replied. And, at this, he plunged in smoothly, instantly toppling her into a dark, dizzying swirl of pleasure that once it began inside her, peaked so slowly that she could only marvel at its ascent.

They lay there together, in each other's arms, until Rose began once more to be aware of her surroundings. They were in the kitchen! When she at last opened her eyes, Rupert was regarding them at eye level with a bemused look on his furry little face, whiskers twitching.

"I guess it's time for dinner," Rose said.

Slowly, they stood up, adjusting and restoring their clothing. Rose, like all women, decided something needed to be said. "I hope this isn't going to set some precedent. I mean, it was wonderful—*wonderful*—but, you know, different meals work on different timing. What if it had been fish in the oven, or a soufflé?"

Karl, wearing an expression on his face not so different from Rupert's, said nothing.

"Well?"

"Rose," he explained, and his tone was loving, if exasperated. "This was about us. And whatever you may think, we're not some ménage à trois with Emeril!"

"Emeril!" she sniffed.

"You know what I mean."

She hesitated. "Maybe."

"Would you understand better if I said you can't reduce me to a side order? Don't you see I'd like to be one-half of the main dish around here?"

Rose found herself giggling. Her cunt still tingled; he was pretty damned attractive, and, after all, he was her husband.

She smiled at him. Then she reached out for his hands. Holding them to her mouth, she tasted the salty skin of his fingers again—and kissed them, one by one.

"You're right," she admitted. She opened the oven door.

"Well, I said it was about us, but I guess it's really more like *The Taming of the Stew*," Karl said.

Would she laugh? In some ways, Karl thought, more hinged on his wife's response to this lame little joke than to his lovemaking.

Holding the stew carefully with two oversized quilted potholders, Rose set it down on the butcher block. "There." She lifted the lid. Steam poured out, its free-floating smells now even more tantalizing.

"You may have forgotten, but I once played Kate at

school." She looked at him gravely. "'I am asham'd that women are so simple to offer war where they should kneel for peace.'"

"I'm impressed."

"You should be.

"No, seriously, you did help. And I *did* remember what you wanted me to. We've been married almost nine years, and, the truth is, you're as precious to me as you ever were. I have no excuse either for taking you for granted or making you play second fiddle to my domestic goddess act."

"Don't go too far. You might regret it in the morning," he cautioned her.

"Karl," she said, "forget Shakespeare. Think Mary Chapin Carpenter."

"What did she say?"

"'Shut up . . . and kiss me.'"

"Only if I can have one of those cheese thingies first. Aren't *you* hungry?"

"Hmmm," was all she said, and reached up to pull him toward her.

VANESSA TAKES WING

❧

by Cansada Jones

"White butterfly
Darting among pinks—
Whose spirit?"
—Shiki

Vanessa peeled the butterfly sticker off the page. *"Nymphalis orion,"* she said softly. Dusky shades of purple fringed in black, with delicate wings highlighted by sharp tips that put her in mind of her ex-boyfriend, Marcus.

Marcus had a sharp tongue and a short temper. You could never win an argument with him. But he was terribly handsome, with dark brown eyes flecked with amber and hands that could be skillful but dangerous, like his tongue. He was also a liar. She sighed, wondering why she had fallen in love with a liar. She affixed the sticker to the back of the birthday card she'd bought for her best friend, Nina. Nina adored butterflies.

Vanessa was giving her a real Monarch butterfly from Mexico. She felt a little sad about it, knowing how swift the life of the butterfly flies by. But Nina had said that's what she wanted, plus drinks and dinner at Hesperia's. A salsa band was supposed to go onstage at eight. Girls' night out. At thirty-three the idea of "girls' night out" still had an aromatic charm. (Like old Indian incense that's almost worn out but if you sniff carefully you can still recall a certain summer night.)

This was so even when the girls didn't have guys they were escaping from, although there was the fact that Nina's last attempt at reconciliation with her ex-husband Dale had failed miserably. Dale had succumbed to the dubious charms of his stick-thin, oh-so-personal secretary who was all of twenty-one and liked to saturate herself with Obsession.

"We're too young to be older women has-beens!" Nina had groaned as she'd given Vanessa last Sunday's "The marriage is still kaput" report over brioches and sugary cafés au lait at Le Pain Brioche.

Vanessa, who'd just attended a Las Vegas wedding for two giddy twenty-five-year-olds, had gotten too drunk at the reception and shoved a blond teenager out of the way so she could grab the bouquet. She understood all too well what Nina was complaining about, but had to appear more optimistic. That's what girlfriends were for—at least, sometimes.

"Speak for yourself, babe. I'm just getting started," Vanessa had said, waving the entertainment section of the paper in Nina's face. "You're only as old as you feel. How are you going to act when you're fifty, like you're ready for the nursing home?"

Nina turned red. "I'm going to be thirty-five. You're only thirty-three! You'll always be younger than me."

"Hey, you've already been married once. I'm still *single* and have never made it to the altar."

Nina had sniffed. "And I'm single again. Maybe forever!" She toyed with the cute butterfly clasp on her trendoid tote, a Kate Spade knockoff by some young wannabe superstar L.A. designer with a New Age complex.

"Oh, be a butterfly! Flutter your wings and be free! Next weekend, remember, we're going for your birthday to that new place with the butterfly stuff on the walls and the butterfly drinks and the butterfly food. I heard they even serve cakes in the shape of butterflies. You've been dying to do this. We'll have so much fun—and there's going to be a salsa band and lots of new people. Maybe we'll meet some guys and hook up . . . who knows? Butterflies have to fall in love again. Right now, we're just in chrysalis form!"

"Fat worm form." Nina had taken another bite of her bun and licked the tips of her fingers. "I think I'll get a chocolate croissant and maybe a loaf of sourdough to go. I'll be good and pass on the chocolate éclair."

"Right."

"Did I tell you that bitch wears her pants so low you can see the crack in her rear peeking out and her midriff never bulges and in the office? He *lets* her do that. What kind of standard does that set in a law firm with major clients? Her shirts *never* cover her belly button, which sports a diamond *he* gave her, no less, in the shape of a heart! I swear to God it's true! Executive assistant, my ass. Executive bimbo's more like it!"

"So skip the chocolate croissant to go," Vanessa said, heading her off at the pass so she wouldn't have to hear the whole sordid and stale story for the umpteenth time. "What can I say? Dale's forty?"

Nina sniffed. Vanessa had prayed she wouldn't start crying again.

"I'm going to start going to yoga classes next week. I think Pilates sounds too hard. . . ."

"Great," Vanessa replied, knowing that Nina would probably attend one week of yoga and then decide that liposuction would be better.

"I think I'm going to make Dale pay for liposuction."

"There you go." Vanessa decided she was really psychic. She promised herself that they'd eat two butterfly cakes apiece for Nina's birthday, if that's what it would take to put a smile on her old friend's freckled face.

❧

So now Vanessa was getting ready to go meet Nina at Hesperia's.

She looked at the old Dover sticker book she'd bought at Half-Price Books. She glanced at the list of butterfly names and smiled suddenly. "Vanessa *io*; Vanessa *clelia*; Vanessa *orithya*; Vanessa *larinia*; Vanessa *laomedia*; Vanessa *amathea*;

Vanessa *charonia*; Vanessa *orithosia*; Vanessa *sophronia*; Vanessa *oenone*. . . ." Repeating the species names gave them an almost hypnotic power. Intoxicating, really. Almost sexual.

Marcus had made her feel so sexual when he first began pursuing her. He'd say he got off just listening to her voice when he'd call for phone sex from one of his out-of-town gigs. Sometimes his voice would turn her on too, and she'd feel goofy as she played along: "Ooh, you make me so hot . . . I'm touching myself . . . lick me . . . kiss me. I want you inside me. . . ."

Sometimes she'd feel like a doofus, grinning, holding the phone away from her mouth so he wouldn't hear her chuckle as he was working his way to orgasm. When did it all go bad? Why did the love she'd felt for him turn to such intense dislike? Did she hate him? Still there were times when she'd catch herself wishing to be swallowed up by him again, feeling his big, always certain cock slide inside her, thrusting, trusting her to take them to that white place flushed with pink light and blue skies threaded with golden rays of pure sunshine delight.

Vanessa sighed again. She hated it when she remembered the good stuff.

She looked at the white box with the chrysalis inside waiting for its transformation and then its quicksilver life. Would Nina watch it birth itself in her bedroom? She gently placed the box and the card inside a pretty gift bag festooned with ribbon and butterfly cutouts.

Hesperia's decor was amazing, and a truly imaginative

tribute to butterflies and moths of all kinds. It could've been a nightmarish version of Hallmark overkill, but the restaurant's owner, a former New Yorker with European investors, had somehow managed to transform a downtown warehouse into a stylish lounge/eatery/cool place to be seen. Even the menu's butterfly food motif came off as witty, as if Hesperia was poking fun at itself.

Vanessa found Nina standing in front of the place looking waifish, despite her protestations that she'd gained twenty pounds after the divorce. Her vintage '60s Courrèges dress fit her perfectly.

"Hi!" Vanessa waved.

A waiter swung open the door just as they approached. And a tall woman wearing lots of jewelry greeted them. "Reservations?"

"Yes, Vanessa Perlman."

She nodded. "Come with me, please." She led them into a cozy room twinkling gently with subdued lighting and sat them in a corner by a window. "Lawrence will be with you shortly. We're very pleased you're joining us tonight!" And would you like Butterflies for two? Or four?" she asked, her voice emphasizing the four, one eyebrow arching.

"Just two for now," Vanessa said. Hesperia's was known for their delectable Butterfly cocktails that purportedly had aphrodisiac qualities even though they were just strongly alcoholic . . . and quite tasty.

"Ah, but later, who knows?" The hostess's other eyebrow arched.

Vanessa looked at Nina but couldn't read her expression. Meanwhile, the woman had vanished, and in her place stood a young man.

"I'm Lawrence. I'll be your waiter for tonight." He bowed slightly and smiled, his white teeth gleaming. His dark, close-cropped hair couldn't conceal its curl, and he looked Italian or Spanish, maybe Argentine. His athletic build accented his tightly tailored pants. Vanessa couldn't help but study the dark hair on the bit of his chest which was exposed. She wondered why he didn't button his shirt all the way and then laughed at herself. Because of women like her? Bigger tip?

He was so hot.

"Great!" Nina said, flirting. "I wouldn't have it any other way, Lawrence."

Come to think of it, Lawrence didn't sound very exotic.

"Where are you from?"

"Everywhere and nowhere," he said, mock-mysteriously.

"I guess he told you!" Nina giggled.

"I'm not being coy; it's just that I've lived so many places. I have an Italian father who lives in Milan, and an American mother who's here in Dallas, but I grew up in New York and Milan mostly. My name is Lawrence Apantesis Sforza. *Apantesis* is a species name for. . . ."

"Yeah, we get it," Vanessa said, rolling her eyes. He had a throaty voice, with an accent that seemed a little fake. "Apantesis . . . sure. . . ."

"Well, do you like our Butterflies?"

Nina had nearly finished hers. She grinned. "How about another round?"

Vanessa glanced at the pale pink elixir. She should've ordered a dirty martini or just plain citrus-flavored vodka. She sipped it gingerly. It was surprisingly good. "I'm fine."

He passed them the menus. "Would you like to hear our specials for tonight?"

Nina smiled sweetly. "Of course!"

As he described the choices, Vanessa distractedly picked at her napkin and glanced at the next table, only to find Marcus sitting there. Marcus and some guy with black-rimmed glasses and salt and pepper hair. They seemed deeply involved in their discussion, as Marcus hadn't even noticed them. Vanessa wanted to put the napkin over her head and die.

Meanwhile, Nina was debating salmon mousse in pastry versus a big thick garlic-stuffed sirloin versus some kind of pasta dish.

Lawrence was watching her. "And you'll have?"

"Salmon Marcus, I guess."

"Excuse me?"

"I mean, whatever she's having—" Vanessa blushed.

"Oh, you should get something different!"

"Okay, the garlic-stuffed penis—"

Lawrence laughed. "That's not on the menu."

Vanessa covered her mouth as she groaned. Did she really just say garlic-stuffed penis?

Marcus had recognized her laugh. He turned, caught her eye, and then looked back at his dinner partner, as if disgusted.

They hadn't parted on good terms. Vanessa, in fact, remembered yelling at him to go fuck himself.

"So I haven't had sex in three years," she found herself muttering. "Is it a crime?"

The sexy young waiter cocked his head. He wore a red stone in his ear that looked like a drop of blood. "That must be challenging," he smiled. "Abstinence can be quite liberating and courageous."

"Just take our order, please." Vanessa wondered if he owned a pair of black leather pants. He probably had three pairs.

"Oysters for starters? Shrimp? Soup?"

"Sure, why not? And goose-liver pâté. Let's go whole hog!"

"And goat cheese?" Nina asked. "Can we have goat cheese after we get some of those awesome Butterfly cakes for dessert? It's my birthday!"

"With Cristal?"

"Oh yeah—and espresso afterward?"

"For such little women, you have big appetites!" Lawrence observed.

"For a waiter who wants a big tip, you have a big mouth."

"Not as big or as luscious as yours, no?" Lawrence replied, outrageously.

Vanessa rolled her eyes. "Our food, please."

"Of course. I'll be right back with the starters . . . and by the way, I *love* garlic."

Vanessa stared into what was left of the pink Butterfly

cocktail by her right hand and nervously smoothed the table-cloth. Nina laughed. A lot. Vanessa could feel Marcus and his friend staring at them. She turned and found that she was wrong. They were gone. Just like that. He hadn't even stopped at their table to say hi. Rude. Just plain rude.

When the food did arrive, they tucked into it with desperate appreciation. It was delicious. The restaurant was filling up, and some tentative music signaled that the band was warming up for their show over in the club area.

Nina was starting in on her Butterfly cake when her cell phone rang.

"Why didn't you turn that off?" Vanessa chided.

Nina waggled a finger and said hello rather loudly. After a few moments, she looked at Vanessa, open-mouthed, pale, startled. "YOU'VE GOTTA BE KIDDING ME!" She shook her head and then snapped the phone off. "Vanessa, I hope you won't hate me, but I have to go."

"What?" The noise in the restaurant seemed to swell at just that moment, and Vanessa found it hard to hear. Nina was saying something about Dale and a reconciliation. That he wanted her back. That he wanted their marriage to work.

That she had to go to him.

She'd talk to Vanessa later.

"Call you later, and thanks so much! What a wonderful birthday! I'm a butterfly—I must fly, fly, to my beloved! Oh, isn't true love wonderful?"

Nina danced out of the restaurant in her strappy sandals, waving her wacky purse behind her.

"Okay," Vanessa started to say when she suddenly real-ized that Nina had left her gift. She stood and tried to catch her, swinging the gift bag, no doubt making the butterfly dizzy. But when she got to the street, she couldn't see which way Nina had gone. She went back inside the restaurant, shoulders slumped, unhappy and uncertain whether to be happy or sad for Nina.

Lawrence was at their table when she got back. "I hope nothing's wrong," he said. He paused.

"Well, here's your check—" he said. He held the cham-pagne in its ice bucket. "I took this off your bill. You don't want it now, I suppose?"

"No," Vanessa said. That was thoughtful of him. It hadn't been opened. Vanessa stared at her own untouched Butterfly cake, "I'd like a take-away box for that, please."

"No problem. But you're not leaving us so soon? You should stay. The salsa band's just about to start. Go on in, and I'll bring you a Butterfly, on the house. "

"And a garlic-stuffed penis to go?" Vanessa surprised her-self, and laughed.

"I'm off in an hour. Shall I join you?"

A pick up by a studly waiter? Things could be worse, Vanessa though. "Okay."

"Go down that hallway—follow the music."

Salsa didn't seem much like butterfly music, but Vanessa was at the point where she'd listen to just about anything, except Nina. She was already dreading the inevitable Sunday morning "marriage" report. Maybe she was just being a poop and it was a good thing, but right now she was tired. Just plain bone tired. She took her drink, Nina's gift and the boxed cake, and headed toward the pungent rhythms, hoping the salsa would jumpstart her aching heart.

She sat at a tiny table listening to the fiery music and watching the dancing couples. She was just getting into it when Lawrence appeared, his shirt even more unbuttoned and his smile wider. He kissed her on the cheek and surprised her with champagne.

"Hmm?" she said, eyeing the ice bucket.

"Just one toast. And then we go for coffee, okay?"

He clinked his glass with hers.

"To three years of abstinence."

"To butterflies," Vanessa laughed.

"Let's go," Lawrence said, after they'd finished the champagne. "I'll drive, and I'll bring you back to your car in the morning."

"Whoa! Who said I'm going anywhere with you and staying the night?"

"I did," Lawrence said, his hand on her waist as he guided them out of Hesperia's without a backward glance.

His car was an old BMW, and its interior smelled of aftershave, pizza boxes and smoke.

"I don't smoke," Vanessa muttered, as she leaned against his shoulder.

"I don't anymore," he said.

They drove through the midnight-blue night, the darkness as velvet as the crayon she'd loved as a child.

"You don't smell like garlic," she said.

He pulled up in front of a small house at the edge of a very rich neighborhood. It looked like it was built in the 1940s and appeared to be well taken care of.

"Wait!" Vanessa said, as he led her into the house. They'd left Nina's gift in the car. "It might be lonely!" she said.

He waited while she retrieved it, then locked his car again. "Come on."

She leaned against him for a moment, then sighed.

❧

Vanessa stirred at 4:00 A.M., staring at the digital clock on the night stand. The bathroom light shone into his bedroom. Was she naked? Had he ravished her? Had there been some sort of date-rape drug in that champagne? She saw Lawrence standing a few feet away, silhouetted by the illumination of the bathroom light—strong, certain and gorgeous. He bent down by the side of the bed. "Are you okay?"

"Yeah." She was wide-awake now.

"Go to sleep. I'll be in the living room. Shall I wake you up—?"

"Wake me up now."

"Excuse me?"

"Wake me up, now!" Vanessa said.

"Oh, I don't think so."

"Don't you want me?"

"Maybe. But on a first date?" He laughed.

"It's been three years."

"Will you still want me in the morning?"

"Maybe."

He crawled into bed. She realized she was, in fact, clothed, and not naked as she had thought.

"To start—" he said, nibbling her ear. His tongue gently probed it, then slid down her neck. (Oh Lord, was she glad she wore her fancy black Victoria's Secret undies instead of her Jockeys.) Then he found her mouth. He kissed slowly, sweetly.

She was surprised. He smelled good. The aroma of the restaurant had vanished. He'd showered. Plain soap. Wet hair.

"I want to get clean," she mumbled.

"Okay!" he said, pulling her from the bed. He gently removed her clothes, picked her up and carried her to the bathroom. Once the shower was on, he soaped her up, and she found herself letting him do all the work. It felt so good. He was a stranger, yet somehow she felt she'd known him all of her life.

His hand slid up her thigh and then vanished inside her, where he pleasured her. Afterward he sighed and said, "What is your name?"

"Vanessa *clelia*; Vanessa *cloantha*; VanessaVanessa *io*. . . ." She laughed then stopped. "Just call me Vanessa."

"Vanessa. . . ." He kneeled down in front of her and the water rained down on his head. He licked and kissed and surprised her with the electricity of his achingly urgent caresses.

"Lawrence." She thought of Lawrence of Arabia, Peter

O'Toole in his prime. She then thought of Ralph Fiennes and Kristin Scott Thomas in *The English Patient*. Would he just go off and leave her in a cave to die?

He probed her mouth again and again. Then he entered her and found passage to the secret place, the place where she truly felt free, like a butterfly released into the air for the very first time.

Spent on the floor of the shower, she felt the water beating down upon her, warm, cleansing and freeing. As he sucked her breasts, she expected honey to drip from her nipples. She sucked his cock and wondered if he would fill her mouth with nectar that would allow her to live a thousand years. She wanted to laugh and cry at the same time. The salt of her tears mixed with the salt of his come, and created an extraordinary ambrosia. She'd never thought of it that way before.

"May I love you?"

"May I breathe? May I eat? May I drink? May I live? " He laughed. "What kind of question is that?"

For a waiter, he seemed romantic but tricky. A man who answers a question with a question is very dangerous. But also, hey, a man. . . .

He toweled her off, wrapped a robe around her, and then they went to his bed once more. She studied him, wondered where his wings would take him next, wondered how long they might fly side by side. There were so many possible routes, and the wind could help, or hinder, their progress. What was their ultimate destination? Was there even a destination? Or just a never-ending journey?

He picked up Nina's present. "May I peek?" he said, his hand diving into the bag. He pulled out the box and held it in his hands for a moment, his eyes wide as a child's.

"No, you'd better not open it . . . *oh*!"

But it was too late. The once chrysalis was now a butterfly, and it had already escaped.

Vanessa smiled.

Lawrence smiled.

Then they kissed again, as the butterfly found an open window.

RISING SON

❧

by Gracia McWilliams

The stranger was seated behind the embroidered screen, hidden from view. But Plum, sensing another presence, and knowing where to look, caught the gleam of light from his eyes in the corner of the room. Her awareness of him sent a delectable sensation rippling from the top of her spine to the soles of her feet as she stepped gracefully into the small, lantern-lit chamber. All of the ladies who worked in the Honorable Madam's house were well aware of the existence of this hiding place; it was used by those gentlemen who wished to take their pleasure through their eyes only.

Plum instinctively knew that the figure sitting there now was not one of the regular watchers. The youthful sparkle of his stare gave him away as Honorable Madam's son who, though he was known to everyone as "Boy," was in fact a grown man. And a very handsome one, too.

Yet Boy always had to remain hidden, for it was forbidden

by law for any adult male to reside in a house of joy. Honorable Madam had taken a heavy risk when she allowed him to return to her household, yet she loved her son too dearly to send him away again. The solution was to instruct her ladies that they were never to mention his presence, nor should they look at or speak to him any more than was strictly necessary. His sojourn now in her establishment was to be a brief one; he would be leaving just as soon as she'd concluded new arrangements for his future.

Plum's blood heated as she thought of the young man watching her. Although she had never spoken to him, she had caught sight of him arriving at the house, and had been impressed by his broad shoulders, noble bearing, and dark, flashing eyes. He had seemed to her like an exiled prince in one of the courtly romances she loved to read. Since that day she had glimpsed him only briefly, but she had passed him once or twice in the shadowy corridors, and the subtle, spicy scent he gave off had made her heart beat faster, as she'd wondered what it would be like to be clasped in his embrace.

It was natural for Plum, who was young and romantic, to be attracted to such a mysterious-seeming figure. Honorable Madam had always spoken proudly of her son in his absence, praising his accomplishments, even reading aloud the poems he sent her. Although he had been born to neither land nor rank, the implication was that he was destined for greatness. And despite the fact that Plum was happy where she was, still she couldn't help dreaming of other adventures.

They might happen, who could say? After all, she was very pretty, with a heart-shaped face, eloquent, melting eyes and a sensual mouth, all framed by long, glossy black hair. These seductive features, combined with a young, supple body and charming manners, had won her many admirers.

Now, all at once, Plum became determined that Boy should be one of them. She wanted to make him long for her favors, dream of her, as she had dreamed of him.

She licked her lips softly in anticipation.

Slowly—very slowly—she began to undress, turning her face away from the screen, hiding the hint of a secret smile.

The well-built older gentleman who had followed her into the room gave a small start of surprise and stared at Plum, his expression containing confusion mixed with lust. This was an altogether unexpected turn of events! Normally, as soon as they were alone, a young lady in Honorable Madam's establishment would simply lie down on the futon and lift her kimono for him. Yet this attractive young lady seemed intent on baring all of her body's sweet curves to his view.

Not knowing what to do, yet inflamed by the novel prospect of seeing Plum unclothed, he waited, his breath coming faster.

Still behaving as if she was alone and with all the time in the world, Plum cast her robe aside, and ran her hands through her long, heavy hair, pulling it forward to hide her breasts and face. Then she combed it back again, lifting the weight of it, only to let it down once more, like a silken waterfall. The luxuriant splendor of her abundant, gleaming tresses had often been praised, and she relished the effect she must be having on both her observers.

Finally, with her face and most of her body still concealed beneath the cascade of hair, Plum lowered herself onto the mattress. She began to stroke herself through her hair, revealing and then concealing the curves of breasts, her slender waist, her pale ivory thighs. With a deep sigh, as if she could no longer resist the temptation, she raised her knees and let her legs fall open. One hand fluttered down to rest delicately upon her sex and, ever so lightly, she began to stroke herself there, wriggling her hips and giving a soft purr of appreciation.

A muffled gasp came from behind the screen. At the same moment, the older gentleman, inspired by her example, hastily began to remove his own clothes—all of them—rather than simply dropping his trousers as a visiting gentleman would normally do. His garments were very fine, Plum noted, and displayed an exquisite taste. She only wished his manners would reflect the refinement of his clothes, and that he would take more care in removing them—not for *her* pleasure, but so she might have more time to display herself to their unseen watcher. That one gasp had been thrilling, but now, although she strained her ears, she could not make out any other sounds over the rustle of falling silk and the heavy breathing of her gentleman.

Her visitor was now naked, and inflamed beyond any thought of restraint. Pulling her legs apart, he efficiently settled himself into place between them.

Normally, Plum would not object. She was not one to linger with a gentleman. Usually, the quicker they found their satisfaction, the better. But now her attention was divided into two, and she wanted the silent watcher behind the screen to receive equal pleasure. Suddenly, with a jolt of dismay, she realized that Boy's view of her was blocked by her companion.

That wouldn't do.

"My dear sir," she murmured. "Don't be in such a great hurry to fell this tree!" She stroked his hardness as she spoke. "Shall we not enjoy ourselves more by tasting the fruit first?"

"Fruit?" he repeated, confused. His mind was not on conversation.

"They call me Plum, you know. Perhaps you see the resemblance?" As she spoke, she was moving sensuously, subtly shifting her position, until now she was directly facing the screen. She shivered with anticipation as she cupped her round little breasts in her hands, lifting them invitingly toward her visitor.

He responded eagerly. Leaning forward, he took one nipple into his mouth. Heat rose within her as he sucked, and she shuddered, feeling herself growing moist with desire. Seldom did it occur to any of her gentlemen to devote any attention to giving *her* pleasure: she had something they wanted; they paid to be allowed to take it. It had always been that way, and, until this moment, when inspired by the silent, watching presence, Plum had never challenged it.

Yet now, as the gentleman moved on to her other breast,

at the same time beginning to fondle the first with his hand, Plum understood that he was enjoying this "fruit-tasting" nearly as much as she. She placed her hands, with their tiny, pink-tipped nails, on his back, gripping him hard to encourage his attentions.

Eventually, after bestowing one final, lingering kiss on each nipple, he demanded, "Now taste *my* fruit!"

Plum was more than willing to comply. It wasn't just the power of oral sex that she enjoyed; she also liked the intimate rush of having her mouth filled with warm flesh, the sheer, primal joy of sucking. At the sight of the gentleman's beautifully swollen cock, she felt the familiar rush of greedy desire, and threw herself down at once to take it into her mouth.

But as she closed her eyes, running her tongue along the warm length between her lips, it was a different face she saw in her mind's eye—and it seemed to be *his* gasps and groans of longing pleasure which she heard. Her own desire quickened, and her head rose up and down, hands and mouth moistening, sliding, exploring, and sucking, always sucking. Abruptly, she had to stop, as her companion stilled her, his hands on her head. His voice was choked as he moaned, "No—no—too good—I'm about to burst!"

She took her mouth away and smiled up at him. "That's all right, my dear sir! Let it come spilling out! I promise, I'll swallow every drop!"

He gave a sigh. "Oh, you are good—so good. But now I want something else. Get up, please, like this." With his big hands he posed her as he wanted her, on her hands and knees, so that now she was facing the screen. How thrilling! She sought out the eyes of the hidden watcher, and they met hers for the first time with an intensity that ignited a flame at the core of her being.

But she saw also that he was alarmed. He worried that she would give him away. Instinctively, she understood everything—*everything*—he was thinking. But could he know that she was imagining him beside her, *inside* her, making her sigh and moan with delight? She imagined kissing those eyes now so close and yet so far away, and willed him to understand that she had been flaunting herself to inflame him, all the while inflaming herself with thoughts of him.

At that moment, the gentleman behind her pushed himself into her and sighed loudly. He began to move rapidly, stroking deep and crying out with each push. Then, with no warning, he stopped, and withdrew from her. A second later, he slipped two fingers into her ass, and then dealt her a sharp smack on one cheek.

"No!" she protested, but softly, so as not to anger him. She worried that things were not going according to her plan.

He began now to move his fingers in a way she found disturbingly arousing. "Why do you resist?" he asked teasingly. "Do you want me to believe no one has ever ploughed this furrow?"

She did not reply, waiting to see what he would do next.

"How does this feel?" His fingers pressed deeper into her.

Still she said nothing. Yet he must have known her answer, for Plum found it impossible to hold back a low moan of pleasure, and, in spite of her wish to resist, she began to rock in a responsive rhythm to the movement of his hand.

She shook her head, trying to refuse, attempting to deny the powerfully pleasurable sensations he was rousing. She raised her head to steal a glance at the embroidered screen, but was distracted by the slow shudders building inside her.

"Trust me!" said the gentleman. "Don't be afraid, my pretty Plum, to taste something new!" He leaned forward to kiss the sloping curve of her back, trailing his tongue down her spine to the place where his fingers probed so expertly.

Plum thought of Boy watching all of this, seeing her like this, and, without meaning to, relaxed. At once she was overcome by the tremors building in her now-pliant body. It was true that she preferred to be in control, and that she preferred other sexual acts to this one, yet here she was, being penetrated against her will—and enjoying it. Knowing that she was being observed heightened her ecstasy.

Yet she had been watched before. Why was this encounter so different?

"That's right!" the man behind her said. "The gates are opening, and I am coming in!"

Her eyes flew to those that watched from behind the screen. She saw that Boy's stare was, if possible, even more burning and intense than before. She knew, again intuitively, that what he was doing was *willing* himself into her very being, and that, somehow, wonderfully, he shared all she felt.

The gentleman reached beneath Plum's body, his fingers

slipping in the wetness there; working in and out, he moved his hand forward until he found her most sensitive spot.

As he touched her there, hot sparks streaked through her, ignited by the circling pressure of his fingers. Any resistance that had remained now evaporated. As he felt her acquiesce, Plum's companion thrust himself hard between her bottom-cheeks, burying himself to the hilt.

Once more, her eyes, staring straight ahead, connected intimately with the watcher's enthralled gaze. As the gentleman began to move himself slowly in and out of her narrow back passage, at the same time stroking an increasingly urgent rhythm with his fingers, Plum's delirium of desire increased.

It seemed to her that she was being possessed at the same time by two different men, and if one had taken her body, the other owned her soul. She was dizzy, panting, torn in two directions at once, and with every stroke, every breath, her desire became ever more powerful and overwhelming, until she felt too small to contain it.

With a shout, the gentleman spurted his seed deep inside her; at that precise moment, the watcher's gaze lost focus, became cloudy, and then his eyes rolled up under fluttering lashes. Seeing this was like that final drop of water which causes the brimming cup to overflow, and, for the first time, Plum came, and came again, in the embrace of a paying gentleman.

Only an hour ago Boy had been bored, restless, indifferent, as he waited for other people to determine his life for him.

Either his mother's scheme would succeed, and a wealthy, powerful man (he had not cared enough even to ask his name yet) would make him his heir, or it would fail, and she would devise another arrangement.

But now, as he gazed from his hiding place at the naked woman lying sated on the mattress, he was transfixed. As he had stared into her dark eyes, watching her writhing in the throes of passion, he'd known that somehow, almost psychically, he had felt everything she had been experiencing. As soon as the exhausted couple began to stir, he slipped out of his hiding place and went in search of his mother.

"Honorable Madam." He bowed low and spoke reverently, but still she looked cross.

"You know you must keep hidden!" Although her tone was scolding, she reached to brush a stray hair tenderly off his forehead.

"Here?" He grinned and gestured around her private chamber, empty save for the two of them.

She sighed. Her son was maddening. Yet it was impossible to stay angry at him, and she always fell prey to his impudent charm. But, thinking of the danger involved, she stiffened her resolve. "Anyone might have seen you! Why aren't you wearing that cloak I gave you?" She sighed again. Really, it was too much!

The cloak was an awful garment, shapeless and coarse. "Madam, your pardon, but not even the lowest peasant would cover himself with such a thing. Here, a rude covering like that might attract more curiosity than the sight of my face. Surely anyone catching a glimpse of me in the passages of your house would believe me a visitor?"

"Perhaps. But our gentlemen know one another. A new-comer always arouses curiosity, and once questions are asked, there have to be suitable explanations."

He waited for her to continue.

"If we are fortunate, you won't have to stay hidden much longer." She stopped to regard him appraisingly. What she saw pleased her; she had done the right thing. "As I told you, I have written to a distinguished and powerful gentleman who was once a favored visitor here, always preferring my chamber for his pleasure. For many years we have had no contact between us, but now I have suggested to him that a handsome young man, through whose veins his own noble blood flows, deserves also to have a name and a position in the world that would not disgrace it."

"Is this fellow really my father?"

"Only the gods are privileged to know for sure," came her reply.

"Hmmm. I've heard it said that the woman herself *always* knows."

"Oh, my darling, don't be naïve. That may be true for a *wife,* but for someone who has led the life that I have, it is a different story altogether. Surely you must see that."

"So why didn't you write to one of them—or even all of them!—at the time of my birth? It is not unknown for a gen-tleman to agree to support his bastards."

She paused before giving him a thoughtful response. "It is

not unknown, but it seldom happens. It's a curious thing, when men have all the power and women exist only as their dependents, that a baby girl has more opportunities than a boy to rise above a lowly beginning. She may make a good marriage, regardless of her name or where she was born. All she needs is for one man to fall in love with her and propose. Especially if she is beautiful. Failing that, she could become a pampered concubine, or have a comfortable life in a superior establishment like this one.

"But for a boy without a lineage, there are no such opportunities. Mostly, they are apprenticed young, sold into a trade, or they join the ranks of the emperor's army. You may say I should have persuaded one of my gentlemen to set me up as his official concubine, but such a desirable arrangement is best made *before* getting with child; no gentleman will give his name to a child he's not certain is his own.

"I took a risk with you, my darling. I decided to play the long game. I sent you away and paid for you to be schooled in all the gentlemanly arts. Indeed, I see you have become every inch the gentleman, your tastes so fine you can't even bear to wear a coarse cloak! I wrote to Lord Higekuro three days ago, to inform him that he had a son by me, that I had raised you by the highest standards, and that he would be proud to see what a fine young gentleman you had become, lacking only the proper name to gain entry into the highest levels of society."

He frowned, sensing a gap in her reasoning. "But why should this Lord—Higekuro?—why should he believe I'm his son *now* if he wouldn't back when I was born?"

"When I gave birth to you, Lord Higekuro was still unmarried. He was devoted to me, and always respectful, but, nonetheless, I deemed it prudent not to suggest to him—nor to any of my other lovers—that I might be carrying his child. However, as the years have passed, although he has wed twice, he suffers the misfortune of having not a single son. His first wife was delivered of two stillbirths before she herself died. His second wife has borne him five living daughters, and two sons who died in infancy. His official mistress is said to be barren. This is a great sadness and burden to him, for although he delights in his daughters and looks forward to the good marriages they will make, every man desires to have a son."

She stopped her pacing and turned to gaze upon him. She gave him a tender smile. "In fact, I have received his reply. Lord Higekuro arrives later this evening, with two close friends. They wish to sample the pleasures of my house. Aftwards, he writes, they will interview me about 'the business' in my letter. So you see, my patience has paid off, and all is unfolding just as it should! When he meets you, you will reveal yourself as the well-brought-up young gentleman that you are, and I do believe that he will invite you home with him. Then, as he grows closer to you, he will want to bestow upon you the power and protection of his name!"

"Now, go!" She made little shooing gestures. "I have things to prepare. Wait until I send for you."

His heart pounded. "Mother—Honorable Madam—I must speak with you."

"Not now! Haven't you been listening?"

"Yes, of course. But this is important—it's about my future."

"Your future has yet to be decided! No, not one word more—not until after your meeting with Lord Higekuro. Now, leave me alone! And stay out of sight, you scamp!"

❦

He had meant to query his mother about Plum, to try to learn about her background, but she hadn't given him a chance. And maybe it was just as well, he reflected, as he bowed reverently and left his mother's presence. His true feelings would have to remain hidden for a little longer, at least until he had a better idea of what lay ahead for him.

He slipped quietly along the corridor that led to various chambers and storage rooms which visitors seldom saw, and entered the dressing room. He would wait here. It was possible that this was the last solitary evening he would have to endure, for if the meeting with Lord Higekuro went well, his whole life might change.

And, if Lord Higekuro did not care for him . . . well, Boy suspected that his mother might have another plan up her wide silken sleeve. It would probably mean having to remain in her house for a few weeks more, or even months, but since his recent encounter with the delectable Plum, that no longer struck him as such a hardship.

If only he didn't have to worry about being seen, Boy thought. If he could somehow conjure a disguise better than his crude, smelly old cloak. Just then, his gaze fell upon the tiers of richly colored robes hanging on a line. He stifled a laugh as the answer came to him. Of course! It was forbidden for any man to live in a house of joy, and an unknown gentleman visitor might be questioned about his origins, but no one would pause to wonder about a woman glimpsed in passing—not even a woman taller than average, with large hands and feet, and perhaps not blessed with a particularly feminine beauty.

Fumbling in his excitement, he stripped off his clothes and selected two of the larger robes from the line. The memory of Plum's smooth ivory limbs and the pink flush of her arousal guided his choice of colors more than any consideration of what they would look like on him. A wig solved the problem of his obviously masculine hairstyle, but as for his face. . . .

Boy frowned at himself in the looking-glass, touching his cheeks critically. No, it wouldn't do. He looked around, but could see no sign of powder or paints. Even if he found them, he knew he might make a mess of it. Face-painting was an art, and not one that he had been taught. Staring into the glass, he noticed that the wig was on crooked. With a sigh, he took it off. He wouldn't fool anybody.

The door slid open. He turned, and the apprehension which had quickened his pulse turned immediately to delight as he recognized the slender figure who had entered.

When she saw him she was startled, and gasped.

"Plum, wait! You're not afraid of me?" His voice was warm and beseeching.

She raised her eyes to his and there it was again, that hot jolt of connection. "You!" she said. A small smile played at the corners of her mouth. "That was you watching from behind the screen!"

"And you knew I was there," he said. Until that very moment he hadn't been truly certain, but now a feeling of joy bubbled up inside him.

She did not reply, looking up at him from under her eyelashes.

He couldn't resist teasing her a little. "I was determined to make the most of my stay here by studying the local customs. Perhaps you could tell me—is it usual in this house for the ladies to disrobe so completely?"

Plum now looked him in the eye and smiled fully. Still she said nothing.

"I thought so," he said, his voice solemn. "So tell me, please, was that exquisite performance purely for your *own* pleasure?"

Now she answered, softly, "For mine . . . and for yours."

"Darling Plum!"

She sighed softly and met his eyes again. "And you, what did you feel?"

"Everything!" he said simply. "Everything."

Hardly aware of it, they had moved closer together. Now he caught her hands and raised them to his lips.

Plum, finding herself awash on a tide of sweetness, swayed. She let her head fall against his chest. As her cheek brushed against the high silk collar of the kimono, and she caught a whiff of a perfume that was not his, she was startled into pulling away.

"What's wrong?"

She blinked. "Why are you wearing women's clothes?"

"I thought I had better disguise myself. I was going to go in search of you, and I didn't want to be recognized."

Putting one hand before her mouth, she began to laugh.

Although it was a lovely sound, he frowned, feeling a little hurt. "What's so funny? I wanted to see you."

Still laughing, she shook her head. "Your disguise wouldn't fool anyone! Anyway, you'd already *seen* me," she added, with a provocative stress on that word.

"Hmmmm. Perhaps 'seeing' was not what I had in mind," he admitted. "Actually, I wanted to do more than just look." As he spoke, he put his hands on her breasts and began to stroke and squeeze them gently through the silk of her robe. Leaning nearer, he murmured in her ear, "Take off your gown. Let me touch you. Let me taste your beauty."

She caught her breath, but then, instead of melting beneath his caresses as he'd expected, she took a step back, pushing his hands aside.

"Wait," she said softly. "You've already seen all *my* hidden treasures. . . ."

Her sudden shyness made no sense to him. Was she going to deny him now, after they had already shared so much? Had he been wrong to imagine that she wanted him as much as he wanted her? He protested, "No, I've only glimpsed them, through the screen."

"A screen that hid you from me."

All at once he understood, and pulled loose the sash of his robe. Shrugging it off, he stood naked before her.

She watched him, and said nothing. But he could see that she began to breathe more quickly as he ran his hands proudly over his splendid nakedness.

"What next?" he demanded to know. "Tell me, do you intend to sit behind a screen and have *me* perform? Perhaps another lady of the house, one of your friends, will agree to my embraces, to help *me* seduce *you*, just as you did me?"

A flash of jealousy narrowed her eyes for just a moment, and then she realized he was teasing her.

She smiled.

"No, I don't need a screen. And you won't need any help in seducing me." She untied her own sash and held out her hands to him.

He came into her arms.

TOUCHING

⊶⊷

by Susanna Foster

It was one of those days when, suddenly, Renny felt as if, all around her, people were following some script she herself hadn't been sent. On the one hand, it was disturbing, and yet, when she thought about it, that wasn't quite right, either. What was happening—and it seemed to be epidemic—was that everywhere she looked people were touching. They were holding hands, kissing, walking arm in arm, embracing— and, alone, she both envied and admired them.

Out on the street, waiting for the bus and in front of the cash machine, hardly anyone was unentwined. Standing in line for coffee and strolling into the park, they were cheek to cheek, hip to hip, elbows interlocked and shoulders leaning lovingly. She hated herself for thinking it, but something Renny also noticed was how many of them were fat, old, or ugly, not obvious candidates for romance.

She was none of those things. Yet there they all were, gazing into one another's eyes, letting a hand graze a cheek in tender appreciation or bestowing a lingering kiss.

So why was no one touching her?

Nonetheless, she knew that she wasn't really upset, or even feeling all that sorry for herself. Despite what they say, not everyone loves a lover. Still, Renny found, more often than not, she did. How could you not rejoice at the spectacle of so much affection being freely demonstrated? It made her more happy than sad to watch all those exuberant caresses, all the hands cupped with bold proprietariness around a familiar bottom, all those he's-mine/she's-mine looks being exchanged.

Renny couldn't even, with any conviction, actually believe that an attractive forty-something woman like herself—gold-streaked hair in a braid down her back, thick-lashed hazel eyes, a generous mouth with a dimple at one corner, and freckles across the bridge of her nose—had any more right to a lover's gaze than someone less comely. In fact, it was somehow better, when you came right down to it, that so many of the touching couples whom she saw touching had probably always been the last kids chosen for teams back in grade school. Life was making it up to them.

These thoughts, in one form or another, occupied her as she paid for a newspaper at the corner stand, exchanged greetings with a bench of neighborhood retirees, dropped her favorite suede boots off at the shoemaker's, bought a cinnamon doughnut and coffee, and slipped some library books into the return chute.

The need to touch: what was it about? Comfort, obviously, and connection. Mothers cradle infants, and dads hold moms. Sometimes it's the same thing, and sometimes it's not. There were moments when you wanted an embrace to satisfy some universal yearning for attachment, and when you could attain contentment simply by coming close to the skin of someone you cared for—and then there were times when that was far from enough.

Women, Renny knew, possess an extra cuddling chromosome. They liked being held, enjoyed the comforts of cozy tenderness and calm stroking. Even right now, as she walked out of the greengrocer's with several large stalks of rhubarb protruding from her black canvas backpack and a carton of strawberries in a paper sack—she planned to make a pie that afternoon—she was trying to remember the last time someone she loved had been touching her.

It wasn't so hard. At least it hadn't been several presidents earlier or back when gas was under a dollar a gallon. In fact, she had actually had a quite enjoyable affair that had ended less than a year ago—more with a whimper than with a bang, middle-aged dating being what it was. But it hadn't been a big deal, either, though at the onset—hormones of any age being what they are—she'd felt that crazy excitement that turns even saggy, baggy fellows into (temporary) Adonises.

The truth was, Henry had been a love, really. He liked eating peanut-butter crackers in bed, did a mean Hoagy Carmichael imitation and didn't mind that she snored. He reread Tolkien every other year, regarding Middle-earth as a destination so real that one might almost send postcards there. Yet at the same time he was also a veteran crime reporter for a city tabloid that daily displayed a rather different notion of fantasy.

Henry would pretend to humor Renny by accompanying her every weekend to the flea markets and church rummage sales she was addicted to, but the miniature delivery trucks and matchbooks from defunct bars that he collected revealed Henry's martyr act to be pure pose. "What bulging pockets?" his mock-innocent look would proclaim, when Renny had more than once felt the sharp edges of the tiny metal vehicles poking in her side as they hugged.

Hugging, people kissing and hugging: that was how this reverie had started. It had been fun to kiss and hug Henry, and even more fun to fuck him, but she hadn't loved him in the way you love people you know have come into your life for Some Important Reason. And so he was history, though not like the Black Death or Custer's Last Stand. Rather, he was decent, friendly history, the kind you could call on the phone and have a cheeseburger with, if you were so inclined.

So what was it she wanted? Men, boyfriends, lovers, guys you met and guys you thought about a lot—they were all the same in the end, even if they tried to pretend they were human. That discouraging conclusion was all she could think of, and she shook her head sadly as she headed up the stairs to her sixth-floor loft.

There was a faithful old elevator, but Renny preferred the exercise when she wasn't carrying too much, and, besides, it was much easier to talk to yourself if you weren't in an enclosed space that, all of a sudden, you might be obliged to share with other people.

"What'd you say? Were you talking to me?"

Renny stopped. Who was that? And what floor was she on, anyway? When she looked at the walls, the peeling paint was unfamiliar, and there was a large, jagged crack next to the window that she'd not seen before. "Oh," she said, trying to recover her lost dignity, "I've passed my floor."

The man who stood a few steps above her thought for a second and said, "I know how it is—it's easy to get distracted when you're having a particularly engrossing conversation."

Renny blushed, considered getting angry, then decided to laugh. "You're right. What's especially satisfying is how I always agree with myself."

"I really don't like to be nosy, but you were saying something about men. I couldn't quite catch what it was, so I'm just going to hope it was flattering."

"Hmmm." Renny couldn't help but notice that he was cute. Men always hated to be called that, and she could see their point. But it was a description that covered everything from movie stars to maintenance men, and, even if she couldn't define it precisely, like all women she knew a cute guy when she saw one.

"I'm Pete, just in case you were waiting until we were introduced. And I'm not an ax-murderer. I'm subletting the eighth floor from Nan and Bob."

"Oh."

"Is that your name? O? Like the novel?"

"Excuse me?" Renny had been thinking about what it was that made some men cute and others not, and so she'd stopped paying attention for a second. "What novel?"

"You know, that French one, by Pauline something or other."

What was going on here? She suddenly felt a little like Alice, except that she'd been moving upward, not down. And Alice had found herself in surreal conversational wrangles with rabbits and caterpillars and bizarro cats, not a cheerful hunk with a passing interest in sadomasochism.

"Oh," she said again. "I mean, that's just what you say, about a million times a day. Oh. I *know* you've heard it before, and if you're going to hold me responsible for conversational placeholders, well, all I can say is I didn't invent them but wouldn't mind collecting a royalty."

"Hmmm," came his reply.

"See."

"But I still don't know your name."

"Why do you need to know it?"

"Because I told you mine, and it's only fair."

"But I didn't ask you to."

"But I'm asking you."

Renny turned to descend back to the safety of her own landing.

"Please . . . no, make that pretty please."

She swiveled and looked at him, suppressing a smile. He

was cute, and this was an unexpectedly entertaining unexpected encounter. Maybe she wasn't Alice, after all, but some postmodern Cinderella. And Prince Charming had moved out of the palace and was skipping the slipper. Why had she been so gloomy about men? Suddenly she couldn't remember.

"Renny," she said. "I'm Renny, short for Mary Reynolds. It's one of those names they give you that are supposed to be said all together, fast, like Billy Bob. I had a Southern grandmother and that was her name."

"But you felt more like a Renny?" He seemed genuinely interested, not just making conversation to keep her standing there.

"Yeah, I guess so. But also, it just happened. Names name you, kind of like cats somehow picking their own."

"Eliot," he murmured.

"If you'd said 'Andrew Lloyd Webber,' I'd have thrown this bag of strawberries at you, and my aim's pretty sharp."

"Listen, if *I'd* said 'Andrew Lloyd Webber,' I'd have had to kill myself, no questions asked. But, given that I didn't, we surely don't have to call the whole thing off."

"Cole Porter, that's good," she said approvingly.

"Anyway, I thought I smelled strawberries. And isn't that rhubarb? Let me guess—a pie?"

"Right in one."

"Can I watch you make it?"

"Just because you know my name doesn't mean you get to hang out in my kitchen. Pies are private things."

"That's crap. If you can make a piecrust that's even half as good as my mother's, I'll marry you."

"How lovely. Such a proposal has never been heard on this staircase. But you obviously guessed my secret—every time I meet a guy named Pete, I remember the little boy who tore the head off my favorite doll when I was four and I have to call my shrink to stop me from eloping with him."

"That's perverse," he said. "And it really turns me on."

"You wouldn't be so hot to trot if you knew what I did to little Pete and how he's been in an institution ever since."

"Ooo, I'm scared."

"Famous last words."

"Honest. I always knew Red Riding Hood was carrying around a bunch of wolf recipes in that basket of hers. What you heard was respect."

"Okay." Renny looked at him carefully now, appreciatively taking in his salt-and-pepper curly hair, well-worn jeans and tanned arms. The sleeves of his soft striped cotton shirt were rolled up above his elbows, and she noticed he didn't have on a belt.

He returned her glance, studying her thoughtfully at the same time.

"I want to touch you," he said, suddenly.

"What?"

"I said, I want to touch you." He grinned. "You know, like 'kiss you 'til your mouth gets numb.'"

"Well, I don't even know your last name, but anyone who can quote the McGarrigles deserves to have a little of his pie voyeurism satisfied."

"What about the touching part? I wasn't kidding about that kissing idea."

"Maybe not. But pie first, kissing later." Did I really say that? Renny had to ask herself. Maybe she'd dreamt this whole thing up, after a morning of thinking about touching and being touched. Besides, why had he used those words? They weren't words people said, often, and certainly not guys in your very own stairwell, even if they were trying to pick you up. *I want to touch you.* She shivered lightly. Plus, who ever got picked up before noon?

"*Belle de Jour,*" he said, breaking into her thoughts. "Did you ever see that?"

Oh, great, she thought. We're back to S and M.

"You remind me of Catherine Deneuve, but warmer, more real. But, hey, forget her! I just realized—Julie Christie. You look just like Julie Christie. And you bake pies, too. Wow."

Renny crossed her eyes and stuck out her tongue. "If it's not my inner self you're after, then forget it."

"Men are cads."

"Frankly, that's what I was thinking, or something close to that, when you started eavesdropping. You might say, this is where we came in."

"Eavesdropping! If you want to know the truth, I've been lurking in every possible corner of this building trying to meet you since I first saw you coming in the front door last week. Didn't you see me panting?"

"Please! Have some dignity."

"None is possible," he confessed mournfully. "It's all behind me now. You will be my Lola Lola."

"I *know* I don't look like Dietrich."

"You don't have to look like her to be my downfall."

"Listen, flattery will get you anywhere, but I'm actually tired of standing out here. You say you're not a serial killer, and, what the hell, I'm going to believe you. But if I'd known someone was going to watch me make my pie, I might have gotten a special outfit—you know, kind of like the old HoJo's logo."

"No funny costumes, please. Or hats. My tastes are simple. I'm sure I'll prefer you wearing nothing, although you look quite nice right now, I hasten to add."

"Nude pie-making isn't my thing."

"Let me be the one to decide that."

"Come on! You're either going to wear me out or wear me down—I don't know which one."

He followed her down the stairs and, whistling "Camptown Races" more or less in tune, waited for her to unlock her apartment door.

Once inside, he did something surprising. Renny was setting the box of strawberries down on the counter when he tapped her on the shoulder. Turning, she heard him say, "Pleased to meet you, ma'am," as he stuck out his hand to shake hers. She let him take her fingers in his—noticing that his own skin was cool and dry while hers felt hot and sticky—and the next thing she knew he was folding her in his arms.

With his lips against her hair, he said, "Mary Reynolds,

you are a woman in a trillion, and I hope you'll let me make love to you before you bake your pie."

She sighed. Why didn't men understand that pie-making was an unlikely postcoital pastime? Still, she said nothing and waited to see what would happen next.

She didn't have to wait long. He pushed her gently away from him, holding her at arm's length while he rested his hands lightly on the tips of her nipples, which were quickly stiffening under her T-shirt. Then, he leaned over, and rubbed his face against one, and then the other. The friction against them was exquisite, and Renny felt the first sensations of that distant yet hovering wave that could, would, might overtake her.

Not yet, she thought, but soon.

He moved away slightly, again, and looked at her. His tone was serious as he said, "I know this must seem wrong to you, on some level. But I think there's another one on which it's very right. I didn't waylay you as an entrapment but as an endearment, for want of a better word, and now I want to prove that to you."

Renny thought it over. Could there be any turning back at this moment? Would there ever be? She leaned over to kiss him. "Pete, it feels a little bit like a dream, I admit. I seem to remember that less than an hour ago, I was leaving my boots down at Angelo's for new soles. And now—forgive me—I feel like a new soul, myself."

He laughed, and she was grateful. It had been a corny thing to say, but she meant it.

He took her hand and kissed it. They walked arm in arm

to the corner of the loft where her bed, covered with soft down pillows and an extra-large duvet, was waiting. She sat down first and he lay beside her. "Will you take your clothes off? I want to watch you."

"I will," she said, and did.

She lay back and he sat, running his fingers up and down her abdomen and teasingly along the insides of her thighs, bending to kiss her breasts, leaning over to lick quickly the arches of her feet and her toes. She sighed first with sensuous contentment, and then with growing arousal.

"Ohhh," she said. "Ohhh. Do that again."

"Like this?"

"Yes. And kiss me."

"Like this?"

A large sigh escaped her as he buried his face first in her stomach and then moved it between her legs. "*Ohhhhh.*"

Wiping his face delightedly, his cheeks still shining with her juices, he sat back a little ways from her, and, with amazing skill, began to rub her clitoris with his finger. Every few seconds he would remoisten it, first tasting her on his skin and then mingling his saliva with her secretions. Faster, then slow. Slow, slow, fast. Where *had* he come from? How could he know her rhythm so well? Slow, fast. Fast, slow.

Stop.

Renny waited, trusting him.

He now inserted a finger inside her cunt, very slowly at first, and then pushing further and harder, circling softly deep inside her, somehow finding places she had never known were there. "Oh," she said. She lacked the strength even to moan. All her energy was concentrated on not losing the momentum he was presenting to her, not falling away from the gift she was being given. Just at this second, he pushed his other hand underneath her and began pressing gently on her asshole. She gasped, unable to help herself. "Oh, God."

He smiled at her, but she barely saw him. He had one wet, wet finger inside her cunt and now another was edging into her from behind. A spasm moved through her, radiating from her center to every extremity, but it was only the beginning. She was rolling and roiling like the ocean during a storm, yet nothing was certain: pleasure would come at her like a cresting wave, and then he would stop—only briefly—just to give her time to strain longingly, with every fiber of her being, toward the tumult once again.

"Renny, Renny," he hummed, as he moved his hands suddenly faster and harder, and then she began to hum with him, though she scarcely knew it. Wet, she was so wet, so very wet. Deep low shudders were gathering inside her as her body stiffened. Wet, she was so wet. *Ohhhh.*

❧

Had anything ever been so sweet, she wondered, as she started to return from the place of no place. She drew her legs up and curled into his body. He held her, kissing her hair and stroking her back. She smiled, though he could not see it, and perhaps, anyway, it was a smile only she knew was there.

This is touching, she thought. And I'll remember it.

About the Authors

Dana Clare admits to spending far too much time on the Internet. She shares a small apartment in Denver with three large cats and a stressed goldfish.

Susanna Foster is a former newspaper columnist who frequently writes about popular fiction. She lives in Baltimore.

Laurel Gross is a writer and television editor living in New York City.

Cansada Jones lives in Texas. Butterflies are one of her passions, and she hopes one day to see the Monarchs on their annual return to Mexico.

Gracia McWilliams was born in Chicago but now divides her time between New York and Japan. She recently completed her first novel.

Mia Mason is a gardener who confesses to a special knack for growing weeds. She lives in the Southwest and also freelances as an artist.

Georgi Mayr is a part-Hungarian, part-Spanish poet and translator. She has worked all over Europe as a language teacher and currently lives in rural England.

Beth Miller is a recovering peanut-butter addict. Her books have been translated into a dozen languages.

Theresa Roland, formerly a journalist in Washington, D.C., now lives in coastal New England with her husband and their assorted livestock.

Susan St. Aubin lives in the San Francisco Bay area. Her erotic writing has been widely published over the past two decades.

Maura Anne Wahl is a native of the Pacific Northwest transplanted to Arizona. She has written occasionally about book-collecting and is now at work on a novel about America during the depression.

Leigh Ward grew up along the Ohio River and is a former bookseller.